FAMILY OF THE DEAD

A ZOMBIE ANTHOLOGY

OTHER LIVING DEAD PRESS BOOKS

BOOK OF THE DEAD
DEAD WORLDS: UNDEAD STORIES VOLUME 1 & 2
REVOLUTION OF THE DEAD
DEAD RECKONING: DAWNING OF THE DEAD
THE MONSTER UNDER THE BED
DEAD TALES: SHORT STORIES TO DIE FOR
ROAD KILL: A ZOMBIE TALE
DEADFREEZE
DEADFALL
SOUL-EATER
THE DARK
RISE OF THE DEAD
DARK PLACES
VISIONS OF THE DEAD

THE DEADWATER SERIES

DEADWATER
DEADWATER: Expanded Edition
DEADRAIN
DEADCITY
DEADWAVE
DEAD HARVEST
DEAD UNION
DEAD VALLEY
DEAD TOWN
DEAD ARMY

COMING SOON

BLOOD RAGE by Anthony Giangregorio
DEAD WORLDS: UNDEAD STORIES 3
DEAD CHRISTMAS: A Zombie Anthology

FAMILY OF THE DEAD

A ZOMBIE ANTHOLOGY

ANTHONY, JOSEPH AND DOMENIC
GIANGREGORIO

FAMILY OF THE DEAD

Table of Contents

ANTHONY GIANGREGORIO

SURVIVAL OF THE FITTEST

The city was nothing but a blasted out ruin of its former glory.

For more than six months the dead walked and the world would never be the same again.

Rodney was one of the few remaining survivors of the human race. This city had been his home and he'd be damned if he would let the walking dead chase him away from it.

So like others hiding here and there, he rummaged through the remnants of a dead city in search of food and supplies, all the while on guard for the dead which now roamed the streets like rats.

Moving from the burned out wreckage of a mini-van to the shattered hulk of an SUV, Rodney slowly made his way down 22nd Street.

Earlier in the week he'd ran into a few fellow survivors. While the two men and one woman wouldn't let him join their group, they did share some information with him and that info was that there was a relatively untouched convenience store on 22nd Street, filled with bottles of soda, cigarettes and canned and boxed food.

The large front glass window was still intact and only the lock on the door had been jimmied. The small group had been there and had then left with as much food as they could carry. For though the store was a find, it was in a heavily populated area of walking dead, and to stay there would have been tantamount to suicide.

Once the dead knew where you were it wasn't long before there were dozens, then hundreds, then thousands trying to reach you.

Picking his way through the rubble, Rodney soon arrived at the convenience store.

His rifle was ready in case there was trouble and a machete hung at his hip for more silent work, but for the most part the street was quiet and he was alone and relatively safe.

But he knew that could change at a second's notice.

At the end of the street, he could see a few shambling corpses meandering about like homeless people once did, but they hadn't spotted him yet. He planned on disappearing before they did.

As he opened the door and stepped into the convenience store, a tinkling of a bell chimed his arrival.

He almost expected to see some Indian fellow pop up from behind the counter and welcome him into the store. But there was no one there of course, nothing but a thin layer of dust.

As he moved through the aisles, gathering food, he couldn't help but smile slightly.

Though there was no reason to be happy in the world he now existed in, he'd learned fast to appreciate the little things in life, such as having food and drink at hand.

It was amazing what the human mind could adapt to if it wanted to survive.

There was a plastic basket on the floor and he used this to drop supplies into as he ate a few candy bars and drank greedily from a can of Coke at the same time. He was still hungry but it took the edge off for now.

Once done, he headed for the front of the store. He planned on returning after he'd stashed his supplies, and as he passed the counter he almost felt like he should toss a few bucks onto the counter top so he wouldn't be accused of stealing.

But of course that was silly. The morals of right and wrong weren't the same as a few months back. Rodney had already done things to survive he would never have imagined possible a year ago.

With one last glance at the empty place, he exited the store, making sure to close the door behind him. With luck, when he returned the next day the store would still be untouched. And with so few remaining Homo sapiens left in the city, he was confident this would be the way of it.

But where the street had been empty when he had entered the store, now there were five zombies coming straight for him. These were the ones he'd seen at the end of the street. Cursing his carelessness for being observed, he made a mental note to be more observant and stealthy in the future.

Though he wanted to just run away from the five ghouls, he knew once they had his scent they would follow him for blocks, so he decided to let off a little aggression and take them down.

His rifle wasn't his first choice to use, as it was too noisy, so instead he set it down with the basket of food and reached for his machete.

Hefting the blade, enjoying the feel of it, he moved towards the zombies.

The first wasn't much of a threat by herself as she was only twelve. The dead girl wore a dirty pink sweater and a dress that went to her knees. She'd been pretty once and Rodney had no doubt all the young boys would have had a crush on her.

But now she was only death walking, and as he moved up to her, the girl opening her mouth wide and hissing, he brought the machete down in an overhand chop that had it splitting her head almost in twain.

The blade was halted in the middle of her face, just above her nose. Her arms were flailing as Rodney tried to pull the machete out of its bone prison with little success. Looking over his shoulder, he saw the remaining four ghouls heading right towards him and he knew only speed would see him through this without harm.

Deciding the machete was in there good, he pushed the dead girl to the street, then stepped on her chest. With leverage now, he yanked up, the machete coming free with a crunch and gobbets of gore and ichor were tossed across the rubble.

The girl was down for good now and he turned to face his next opponent, a geriatric Chinese man with wisps of white hair fluttering in the breeze. He was so ancient at first Rodney wondered if the man wasn't a zombie, but was perhaps pretending, but when the old man looked at him, Rodney could see the same milky white eyes he had come to hate.

With a yell of revulsion, Rodney slashed at the old man's face then spun the machete around and jabbed it into the ghoul's left eye. The milky white orb was pierced and the blade slid deeper as the ghoul danced like a puppet.

Using his foot again, he kicked the old zombie to the street, the machete sliding out of the eye socket. Metal grated on bone and he cringed, the sound filling him with something like when a teacher scrapes her fingernails against a chalkboard.

With the old man now down, he ran a few feet away to give himself some clearance and then turned to face the last three zombies,

The third was a middle aged man wearing a t-shirt with a picture of a clenched fist and the words. **Want an Irish Kiss?** printed in bold letters. He had a beer belly and a balding pate and his face was almost entirely gone, only the red and black of the underlying rotting tissue prevalent. Insects and flies crawled about the ghastly wound, feeding on the walking corpse.

Disgusted, Rodney ran at the zombie and slashed with his machete, taking off the ghoul's right hand at the wrist. No sooner did he do this then he was slashing at the remaining hand, both dropping to the street to lay forgotten.

Ichor seeped from the jagged stumps but the ghoul wasn't deterred in the slightest.

Rodney took a step backwards as the other two zombies moved on him and he scrambled over a pile of rubble.

When he was in a clear area again, he picked up a three foot piece of rebar out of a pile of shattered reinforced cement, and with a grin, waited for the bald zombie to climb over the rubble.

When the zombie was halfway to him, it slipped and tumbled down the incline to sprawl at Rodney's feet. Pleased with his good fortune, Rodney raised the rebar and brought it down hard, the tip of the metal piercing the forehead and into the brain within. Twisting the rebar, he made sure the zombie was out of action, then turned to face the last two ghouls who had simply walked around the pile of rubble instead of trying to climb over it like their unfortunate brother.

The next zombie was a young woman in her twenties, or had been. She was naked as the day she was born. Even in death, with wounds and bite marks across her body, he could see she was an attractive woman. Her pendulous breasts, now pale, with veins prominent in them, swayed as she walked, and her dark mound of pubic hair had small insects crawling around between the follicles. Her hips were curved and her abdomen was flat, muscles hard and tight. Her blonde hair, once perfectly groomed, was now a matted and tangled mess of gore where flies and other flying creatures swarmed and lived.

But despite this she was still beautiful.

Her cheekbones were high and her eyes were wide, though the deep blue had long faded to white. She had a perky nose and manicured eyebrows and Rodney imagined her on a runway somewhere, strutting around wearing today's latest fashions.

Or was that yesterday's latest fashions?

She was the first of the duo of the two zombies arriving, and behind her, the dead frame of what had once been a male soldier, complete with bloody fatigues.

He couldn't help but wonder if she wasn't a mindless corpse, if she was still capable of reasoning power, just what she would think of her present predicament, walking around the city naked for all to see her goodies.

He could only hope if he ever ended up as one of the walking dead that he would at least have a little more dignity.

To walk around to the end of the time with your ass hanging out, now there's a sobering thought.

Well, whoever she had been in life and no matter how she looked, now she was the enemy who would rip him apart and feed on him if given half the chance.

Raising the machete, Rodney moved to meet her and took her head off with one powerful swing. It was something he was wont to try, but today he felt over confident.

The blade sliced through the dry skin and sinew like a hot knife through butter and her head bounced away like a run away soccer ball to land on its side in a pile of rocks. A geyser of black blood shot up and out of the jagged neck stump catching the light of the day.

Idly, he was always amazed at this result whenever he took off a limb. If the zombies were truly dead, then how could blood still pump through arteries and veins now immobile? For blood to pump a heart needed to be beat and if so, would that mean the dead weren't truly dead?

These and other ruminations were cut short when the dead soldier came at him. If the soldier was bothered that Rodney had destroyed his woman sidekick, he gave no sign, his face filled with the same blank stare.

Rodney knew he needed to finish this fast. He'd been in the area too long already. With the commotion they were making, it was just a matter of time until more of the dead things made their way to his location.

The soldier growled low in his throat and lunged for him, but Rodney stepped nimbly aside and swung the machete. The blade took the dead man's left hand off at the wrist, more black blood shooting out like a garden hose set to high.

Laughing a little with the ease of the battle, Rodney grew over-confident, and when the soldier turned to attack again- unfazed at the loss of the limb- Rodney swung the machete again.

The blade sank into the zombie's upper arm, but instead of slicing clean through, Rodney's blow wasn't powerful enough and the blade became lodged in bone.

A look of panic came across his face, and as he tried to decide what he should do, the solider reached out and wrapped pale fingers around Rodney's throat with his one remaining hand.

The dead man was bigger than him and the hand squeezed around Rodney's neck like a vice as the fingers sunk deep into his throat, causing him to see spots of yellow and white.

And then, to Rodney's shock, the zombie began to lift him into the air, his feet now dangling a few inches off the rubble strewn ground.

Rodney let go of the handle of the machete and both his hands went to the arm now holding him in thrall as the other, handless arm, seemed to be punching his abdomen. With each blow a black stain was left behind and Rodney could smell the foul stink of the viscous fluid that was considered blood for the zombie.

Rodney became filled with panic as he tried to suck in one more mouthful of air, but the grip on his throat was too strong and he felt himself blacking out.

In that brief flash of an instance between losing consciousness, he heard the report of a powerful gun and watched the zombie's head explode, like a stick of dynamite had been shoved into its ear and then lit.

He felt his face and arms sprayed with bone fragments and gray matter, the wet slapping sound filling his ears and a feeling of disgust as the gore caressed his skin, but then he slid into the dark void of oblivion and knew no more.

*   *   *

"Hey, buddy, you all right? Come on, man, get the hell up. We have ta get outta here."

Rodney heard the words as if he was in a long tunnel and the speaker was at the opposite end from his location. The voice was also muffled, like the owner was under a blanket or pillow.

Rodney's eyes fluttered and he parted them a bit, still groggy from losing consciousness, and at first he didn't understand where he was or what had happened. But then his eyes took in the shape of a man standing over him and his eyes went wide, fearing a zombie had snuck up on him.

Rolling to the side and reaching out with his hands to get to his feet, his right hand sank up to the wrist in the remains of the soldier zombie. The cool brains felt like cold spaghetti under his palm and he yanked his hand back with revulsion, the taste of bile already touching the back of his tongue.

The man standing over him knelt down and placed a comforting hand on his shoulder.

"Easy there, partner, just slow down, you're safe for the moment."

"You, you can talk?" Rodney said as he shook his hand clear of brown and black goop.

"Sure can, why, that something new ta ya?"

"No, I...uhm, what I mean, I thought you were one of them, you know, dead. It's just, I haven't seen another living person in a while and..." Rodney drifted off then stopped, realizing he was rambling.

"Same goes for me, too. You're the first live human I've seen in quite a spell." He held out his hand to Rodney who was still sprawled on the ground. "Names, Jed, Jed Manners."

Rodney reached out to take the proffered hand and realized he was going to use the one covered in brain bits, so he quickly switched and shook the hand with his clean one.

"Rodney."

Jed motioned if Rodney wanted help getting up, and with a nod from Rodney, Jed yanked him to his feet. Jed was a large man with wide shoulders and a beer belly. He had a hard face with a few days worth of stubble and a scar on his chin, looking so old he may have received it when he was a child. Rodney had never been a good judge of age, but Jed appeared to be in his late sixties or early seventies.

A low moan carried on the wind and Jed glanced over his shoulder to see the shapes of zombies as they worked their way through the rubble.

"Damn, there's more of 'em. Look, buddy, it's time to vamoose from here. I got a place a few blocks over, it ain't pretty but it's served me well for a while now. If you want, you can come with me, stay for dinner. I've got plenty of food, meat, too. After that we can take it a second at a time."

Rodney could see the shapes as well and knew it was time to leave. With nowhere else to go and glad to see another living being, he agreed.

"Oh, wait, I got some food, too," Rodney said as he went to retrieve his basket from the convenience store.

Jed slapped Rodney's back jovially, turned, and headed off, Rodney following right behind after he picked up his rifle, the food and machete. As they moved through the wreckage, Rodney saw a few more fresh corpses scattered about the street that weren't there before. Evidently while he was out cold, Jed had done some cleaning up. The man had protected him, had watched over him, a perfect stranger. That wasn't at all what he would have expected. Since the dead began to walk most people had become even more selfish, especially as food supplies and the power had dissolved.

Rodney's stomach was growling even more now in anticipation of eating meat.

He assumed it would be rat or cat, as most of the dogs were long gone or had been eaten by man or the dead.

Still, it had been days since he'd eaten anything he could call a *true* meal. Which of course had him imagining what Jed had waiting for them back at his hideout. Rodney imagined cans of fruit, beef stew and chili as well. Boxes of juice and maybe even bottles of beer. He would kill for a bottle of beer, Hell, he'd drink it warm, wouldn't matter at all.

Jed led him deeper into the city, the man not talking, his eyes alert for danger.

Every now and then a zombie would pop up from an alleyway or from behind a car or truck, but either Jed would shoot it down or they would simply outrun it.

In no time Jed slowed at a destroyed building with a crumbling façade. A few destroyed cars and a bread truck lay scattered on the street like giant Matchbox cars left by a bored child at the end of playtime.

Jed pushed a large piece of plywood aside and gestured for Rodney to enter first. There had been a small piece of red brick on the top of the plywood, wedged between the building and the edge. Jed had studied this before moving the wood.

Rodney hesitated, looking at Jed. The gaping hole in the building the plywood had hidden was so black it resembled a massive pool of ink and his mind raced with what might be waiting for him on the other side.

"Go on, there's nothin' in there that's gonna bite ya. This piece of wood and the brick was right where I left it."

Rodney nodded, understanding immediately. If the brick had been moved or wasn't in the exact same spot as before, Jed would've known someone had been inside his sanctuary.

Rodney, now more confident, nodded and entered the hole, Jed directly behind him. As Rodney shuffled a few feet away from the hole, his eyes adjusted to the gloom and he realized he could see what little there was to see. But then Jed entered and pulled the plywood back over the hole, thus blocking out what light had been seeping in.

Rodney felt his heart flutter in panic, the darkness not his friend, but then Jed flicked a match and the darkness was banished once more. The man grabbed a makeshift torch from a barrel set to the side of the hole and lit it, the flame like a miniature sun as it filled the area around Rodney with yellow light.

With the darkness banished, Rodney saw he was in an underground parking garage, complete with vehicles still parked where their owners had left them. The only difference now was the inch layer of dust coating each car and truck like a blanket.

"This way, right this way," Jed said and moved off, walking comfortable, a man who knew he was safe in his own home.

Rodney followed, the rifle slung over his back and the machete still in his hand, but now forgotten. If anything came out and tried to jump him, both he and Jed could deal with it easily.

Jed weaved though the maze of cars until he came to a small camper parked in the middle of the deserted lower level. The top of the camper was inches from the ceiling of the garage and Rodney mused at how the owner must have been biting his nails in worry as he'd driven through the entrance to the garage.

"Here we are, home sweet home," Jed grinned and opened the side door to the camper. "After you."

Rodney nodded, not worried in the least as he moved to enter the camper. And why would he be? Jed had saved his life after all. If the man had meant him harm, there'd been a hundred places where he could have attempted it, not the least of which was when Rodney was sprawled on the ground unconscious.

So when the blow to the back of his skull filled his vision with white light and he went head first onto the top stair of the camper, his mind's only thought was why this was happening, because every reason why made no sense.

Jed conking him on the head was irrational.

And that was the thought he took into the darkness as his mind tumbled back into the void.

*　*　*

Rodney didn't know how much time had passed, but it felt like more than an hour and less than a day, as he slowly came back to consciousness for the second time in what was a matter of hours.

When he tried to sit up, he realized his arms and legs were tied to something. Turning his head from side to side, he found himself to be on a makeshift platform.

No, not a platform, a door, a wooden door propped up on two saw horses.

A torch burned silently a few feet away, casting a small circle of light around him.

Struggling for a few minutes, he found he wasn't going anywhere, he was stuck.

Looking through his feet, he could see the camper sitting quietly.

So he was still in the parking garage.

Then he remembered being hit and it all came back to him.

Jed.

Jed had knocked him out. But why?

"Hello! Hello, anyone there? Jed? Why am I tied up?"

At first there was no answer, no sound other than his echoing voice. He felt so helpless strapped to the table. A zombie could come out of the shadows and there would be nothing he could do.

And then he saw the camper's weight shifting on its shock absorbers, as if someone was walking inside it, and a muffled voice could be heard.

After another few seconds, he heard the distinct sound of the camper door opening and then footsteps as someone approached him.

No, wait, there were two people approaching him, though the second one seemed to be a wisp of a thing, half the size and shape that was Jed.

Jed seemed to be leading the second shape along, and when the two people reached the edge of the small perimeter of light, Rodney let out a gasp of shock.

Jed was there, of course, but it was what he was leading by a leash that was so startling.

It was one of the dead, a shriveled old thing that even in life would have resembled a zombie.

Jed slowed when he reached Rodney who was even now struggling in vain to get free.

"Momma, this is Rodney, he's come over for dinner tonight," Jed said, his eyes filled with more than a touch of madness.

Rodney could feel a tightness in his bowels and his heart skipped a beat.

"Jed, what's going on here? Let me up, untie me, man, please. And what the hell are you doing with that *thing*?"

Jed's face grew cloudy with anger and he reached over and slapped Rodney on the face.

"That's my mother, damn you, not *thing*, and you best watch your mouth."

Rodney realized Jed wasn't all there and his best chance of getting out of his present predicament was to try and sweet talk the man; gain his trust so he would let him go.

All the while the old woman was straining at the leash, but she was so small and frail she was like a feather in the wind. Rodney also saw she wore a gag so she couldn't bite anyone.

"Okay, sorry, she's your mom. So, what's she doing here?"

Jed smiled then, a manic smile that had Rodney pissing his pants in fear. As Jed spoke, he was removing the gag from his mother's mouth. Then he reached into his pocket, pulled out a pair of dentures and popped them into her mouth with practiced ease.

"Like I just said before, Rodney, you're here for dinner. But I think you misunderstood me. You're not here for *your* dinner; you're here for Momma's."

And with that he dropped the leash attached to his mother and let her move forward, directly at Rodney who was as helpless as a human could be.

"But if you just wanted to feed me to her then why didn't you just knock me out in the city? Why did you wait till we got back here?"

Jed shrugged. "That's simple, I didn't want to drag you all the way here and I couldn't carry you seems my back is shot. It was easier to just get you to come on your own and then sack you when your back was turned. Now shut up and let momma eat. She likes peace and quiet, says it's better for the digestion."

Rodney had time for one good scream as he felt the sharp dentures of the old woman tear into his throat. He could feel his blood pumping through his carotid artery and into the old woman's mouth with each beat of his pile-driving heart.

Slowly the pain began to fade as his senses became dulled and he managed to hear Jed one last time as he spoke a few last words to him.

"Sorry, buddy, but it's dog eat dog out there now. Survival of the fittest and all that. I loves my momma somethin' fierce and she's gotta eat. So I gotta..."

Rodney didn't hear the rest of Jed's words, and he never would.

All the while Jed talked, his mother feasted on his now cooling corpse.

And why wouldn't she?

Rodney was a meal fit for a king.

JOSEPH GIANGREGORIO

MOTHER DEAREST

Kyle Tucker was returning home after a long day of work at the funeral home, his mother sitting next to him in the passenger's seat. He had been working there for the past four years as a coffin handler, making sure which one goes where throughout the building, just to pay off his student loans and apartment, the latter being in his mother's basement.

Yes, she charged him rent.

The reason why he got the job over other applicants was simply because his mother owned the funeral home.

Kyle was just a typical, twenty year old guy who just wanted to cut the imaginary umbilical cord that was between him and his mother.

His mother's name was Liz, and she deeply loved her son and never wanted to hurt him. She also never wanted him to stay out too late or too go too far on dates. She had explained to him that women were hussies and gold diggers who were looking for a man to take care of them.

That was one of the reasons why Kyle got the job in the first place, because his mother didn't want him to go off and get another job and end up getting hurt or taken advantage of.

Kyle could describe his mother in one word, and that would be *zombie-like*, because Liz, even though she was fifty, had too many wrinkles on her face from smoking earlier in life. The cigarettes probably had taken five years off of her life if not more. She had short, curly blonde hair (dyed of course) and a voice that sounded like she had a frog living inside her throat. Kyle thought that her voice was the most annoying voice in the world.

As Kyle was about to turn onto his street leading to his house, Liz finally spoke up, just to nag him once again, though she had been doing it all day at the funeral home.

"You know, Kyle, you were awfully quiet during this car ride and I've been getting complaints of you not doing your job correctly. Why is that?" Liz asked curtly, though she already knew the answer. She had a habit of doing that to him; asking him questions when she knew the answer.

"Because, Mom, I want my license and it's aggravating. I can't keep driving with you in the car all the time. I've got a date this weekend with a girl that I met at the funeral home. She was a customer actually. Her grandfather just died." He sighed. "I wish Dad was still alive, he could teach me to drive and I could get the real thing, not this stupid learner's permit," Kyle said as he pulled the car into the driveway of their home.

His father had been his best friend until he died from a heart attack when Kyle was thirteen, and that was the reason why Liz had been babying him and would never let him out of her sight.

"No, you're not going on a date. I've got to be at the funeral home this weekend for a wake and funeral and you'll be working all weekend, too," Liz said, making an annoyed face.

"That's crazy, Mom," Kyle said, "I'm twenty years old, for God's sake. Who doesn't have a car, let alone a license at twenty? So, guess what? Tomorrow, you and me are going to the DMV, even if I have to drag you there by your hair," he said, turning off the car and stepping out.

"Kyle, watch your mouth with me! I'm your mother, dammit. You're my son and if you live under my roof you'll follow my rules, and on that note, you're grounded for the rest of the night," she said, getting out of the car.

"See what I mean?" he said. "I'm twenty and you treat me like I'm still thirteen. You can't ground me, Mom, I'm a grown man. An adult if you ever bothered to really look at me."

"Not to me, dear. To me you'll always be my little boy."

Kyle was walking away now and Liz was trying to get the groceries from the back seat by herself.

As Kyle was entering the front door, she called out to him.

"Kyle, where are your manners, get back here at once and help with these things," she said.

But Kyle wasn't hearing her. Unlocking the front door, he stepped inside, and in his aggravation and rage, slammed the door closed, and by doing this, he hoped to drown out his mother's voice for just a little while.

*   *   *

Later that night, Kyle was lying down on his bed, listening to his AC/DC cd, with his mother upstairs, making dinner. Kyle was deep in his thoughts, thinking of how he hated his mother with a passion, but until now, had never had the urge to act on his emotions. He had visions of killing her, of strangling her till her face turned blue. But then something snapped inside him. Whatever had always stopped him, whatever conscience had kept him in control, suddenly melted away.

He decided finally that tonight would be the night.

As he was looking at his prized sword collection that he'd been collecting for years, he was thinking that he could just cut her head off with one swipe of one of the swords. But no sooner did these murderous thoughts fill his head then reason returned and he thought otherwise, knowing he wasn't a cold blooded killer.

And come on, he was talking about his mother here; he couldn't kill his mother, could he? Sure, she treated him like shit, but come on, it was his *mother*.

"Kyle, time for dinner!" Liz yelled. "Oh, and I was thinking. Maybe this weekend I can figure out a way so you can go on your date. But I want to come too to make sure you don't screw it up."

That's it! he screamed in his head. What his mother had said just pushed the kill button in Kyle to the ON setting. She had been doing this for years, plus many other things to belittle and control him, and now he couldn't take it anymore.

For Christ's sake, he was only human. How much could one man take?

Kyle turned off his AC/DC cd and rolled off his bed to grab one of the swords that was hanging peacefully on his wall, but tonight, it would finally be used. With sword in hand, he slid the blade out of the sheath and inspected it. He rubbed his index finger across the blade on the side, the long ways, and saw that it was in great condition. He also realized it would be more than sharp enough to cut his mother's head clean off.

"Kyle, you have thirty seconds to get up here, or you're going to bed without dinner!" she yelled again, treating him like he was ten.

"This is all or nothing," Kyle whispered as he quietly climbed the steps one at a time. No more would she belittle him and treat him like he was a child. It would all end now.

As he approached the door that would open into the kitchen, he peeked through the small crack between the door and frame to see his mother already sitting down at the table, her back facing him.

Nodding to himself that this was something he had to do, Kyle quietly opened the door so his mother wouldn't hear him. Sneaking up from behind, he approached his prey. He tightly held the hilt of the sword with two hands and raised it high and to the side, ready to swipe it downward.

But then he stepped on a squeaky floorboard. That was when Liz quickly turned around to see the blood lust and rage in her son's eyes, and with one fluid motion, he brought the sword down and to the side, slicing her head off and separating it from the rest of her body.

The sword never stopped, easily cutting through the spine, and the skin was obviously easy, almost like cutting through butter. As the sword came out of the other side, Liz was taking her last gasps of air and then her head tumbled to the floor and rolled away from the kitchen table.

Blood began to shoot out of the neck hole that was where Liz's head used to be, a scarlet spray that splashed everywhere, including the ceiling. In seconds, warm plasma was all over the kitchen and on Kyle, the coating warm and sticky.

Kyle was in complete shock, not realizing how gory and messy it would be, and he stood there for a good five minutes, blood dripping off the tip of the sword. Another few minutes went by and then Kyle suddenly snapped out of his state of shock, realizing that he had to hide the body. No matter how he now felt, whether it was regret or joy, he couldn't leave her like this in the kitchen.

"Shit, now what? I can't let anyone see this," he said to himself, as he tried to think of an idea of what to do with his mother's body.

Then he realized he could stuff the body in the chest freezer downstairs in the unfinished part of the basement, right next to his room. But he knew the body would be a tight fit until he thought that he could then put the severed head in the extra refrigerator that sat next to the chest freezer.

He decided that would be the best course of action for now. Before he informed the police she was missing, he would have to get rid of the body, but for now it should do nicely.

Not wanting to touch her still twitching form, he went and retrieved a pair of latex gloves from under the kitchen sink, then got to work.

After wrapping the body in a couple of black plastic bags, he picked her up and placed her over his shoulder in a Fireman's carry, all the while holding his mother's head by her hair, the head swinging back and forth like a ball on a string.

Descending the stairs to the basement, he reached his room, and at the opposite end there was a door that led to the rest of the basement. He opened the door with his free hand and quickly walked over to the chest freezer, dripping small drops of blood in his wake. He then opened it and threw the fresh corpse inside amongst the pot pies and fudgecicles, making sure it would fit in there by moving a few items around and setting others on her body. As an after thought he grabbed a fudgecicle for himself, relishing in the fact that if she was alive she would be bitching at him right now about it.

To make sure it was cold enough, he turned down the temperature, not wanting to take any chances.

After dealing with the body, he then picked up the severed head and went over to the refrigerator. This fridge had both a freezer and a regular refrigerator in separate sections. It was the old one from upstairs, but when they got a new stainless steel one, they placed the old one in the basement for a backup.

Opening the freezer door, he quickly took all the ice cream out and everything else that was in there so the head would have enough room. As he set the head down, he turned down the thermostat so the freezer would be colder than normal, wanting the head to be preserved, then closed the door.

With the body and the head now dealt with, he now had the chance to do all the grunt work of cleaning up the kitchen of all the blood splatter.

He then headed back upstairs to get to work.

As he stepped onto the first floor, he realized the clock on the far wall read 8:30 pm. Not wasting anymore time, he grabbed a couple rolls of paper towel and got to work, and as he cleaned and scrubbed he went over in his mind what exactly he would tell the police.

Three months later.

Kyle was just waking up from a good night's sleep. As he rubbed the sleep out of his eyes, he saw the calendar on the wall and remembered that it had been nearly three months since he'd killed his mother. As he lay there, he thought about all the paper work he'd had to do to become the legal heir to the family wealth. From getting the deed of the house to be put under his name, to being the new owner of the funeral home, even though he didn't know how to run one, to filling out the police paper work when his mother had been documented as missing.

Despite the fact he had lived in the house alone for the past three months, he still stayed in the basement. He liked it, to him that was his home, not upstairs.

As he rolled out of bed, he remembered the story he had concocted to tell the police. First he had played the dutiful, concerned son, then had filled out a missing person's report. They said that after an extensive search they ruled Liz might have run away with someone during the night she went missing. Of course this was helped by Kyle mentioning he thought his mother was seeing someone though he didn't know who.

When the police finally summed it up as an unexplained missing person, Kyle was so relieved he didn't get caught after committing the murder he almost collapsed on the floor. After all, with forensics and DNA, no one got away with murder anymore.

But there was another reason why the police had dropped his mother's case, when in other times they may have continued dogging him, wanting to see if Kyle was hiding anything.

As he was walking up the steps to the first floor, he heard an intensive banging coming from the front door.

"It seems like there at it again," Kyle said to himself casually.

As he walked into the living room, he saw that the curtains covering the large picture window were still closed from the night before, so he went over to them to let some sunlight in. When he reached them, he quickly pulled them apart to see through the only section where there weren't wooden planks covering the glass.

As he peered through the slits in the boards, he could see the same bunch of zombies roaming around. This group had arrived a few days ago and just wouldn't leave him alone.

The zombies first began arriving about two months ago. They seemed to appear out of nowhere, but the police and experts said it could have been bacterial or viral that spread quickly among the hosts. At the same time the dead began to wake up, a flu-like virus began to spread through most of the country. The virus killed fast and then whatever was doing it would change the fresh victims into walking cadavers or what everybody had no choice but to call them...*zombies.*

Others thought it was something else, radiation or the ozone or a million other ideas. Some said the dead walked because it was the Rapture and God was punishing everyone for the sins perpetrated in his name.

The truth was, no one really knew why the dead began to walk.

As Kyle was watching this, he saw that the entire street was filled with the walking dead and he knew he wouldn't be going anywhere for quite a while. When this plague first started, Kyle decided to get a lot of nonperishable food, knowing he would be stuck in his house for a long time. He then got wooden planks from the backyard and started to board up all the doors and windows, except for the front door, knowing it would be sturdy enough to hold an attack of even a dozen zombies. Besides, he needed some way out if it came to that.

When the zombies saw his shadow as he peered out the window, they quickly began to move towards the house and that was when Kyle decided to close the curtains and get some breakfast. He knew they would get bored and move away, back to the street after a while.

When he went into the kitchen, a voice floated to his ears. This voice had been calling to him since the zombies first came out. He'd been ignoring it ever since it started, but with each passing day it grew harder to ignore.

Trying to focus his attention on something else, anything else, he poured himself a glass of apple juice.

"Kyle, Kyle, where the hell are you?" the disembodied voice called. "Come help me!"

Drinking half the juice, he turned and looked at the back door. A few shadows were there, more of the dead trying to get in.

Placing the glass of juice on the counter, he started to inspect the house to make sure it was still secure. Sometimes the zombies managed to get the boards off and he had to sneak out and fix them at night when they couldn't see him. He had to be fast for once he started pounding nails, they would hear him and come his way, but they were slow and it didn't take long to fix the boards and escape their clutches.

After checking the first floor and satisfied it was still safe, he heard the voice yet again.

"Kyle...Kyle, I want you to come here right now!" the voice said.

Kyle decided he'd ignored the voice for long enough so he went downstairs to the basement, into his room and through the door leading to the other half of the cellar.

"Get me out of here, Kyle, it's freezing in here," the voice said, though slightly muffled.

"I don't believe this is really happening," Kyle said to himself, knowing exactly where the voice was coming from. When he approached the freezer door of the refrigerator and opened it, the voice sounded loud and clear.

"Kyle, it is you. Get me out of here, now!" the voice snapped.

Kyle did nothing, said nothing, he just stared at the severed head of his mother. Liz's face was freezer burned, a few ice crystals built up on her nose and ears. Her face was covered with ice and her lips were cracked from the frigid temperature. Her eyes were wide and moving and her tongue, though stiff, slid out of her cracked lips as she stared at her son accusingly.

"Mom?" Kyle said.

"Kyle, my God, look at you. You look like hell, what happened to you?" Liz asked from inside the freezer. "And what happened to me? Why am I in here? I don't feel right. Where's the rest of me?"

"I...I...don't know, you see I kind of..." Kyle paused, not wanting to tell his mother that he'd killed her.

"I know what you did to me, Kyle," Liz said firmly. "You chopped my head off. Anybody with half a brain or even somebody with no lower body can figure that one out. How could you do that to your own mother? Are you some kind of a monster?"

"I...I. Aww, Mom, sheesh," Kyle said, suddenly feeling very guilty about what he'd done to his mother.

"Forget about that now. Quit standing there with your hands in your pocket and get me the hell out of here," she demanded.

Falling back into old habits, he did what he was told, reaching in and picking up the head like it was a rump roast. Liz's mouth opened slowly, her teeth visible, and Kyle halted, wondering if she was going to bite him.

"Oh, don't worry, Kyle, I won't bite you," Liz said, calming her son down.

Kyle nodded at what she said, and though still careful, he shifted his hands and grabbed her quickly by her hair.

"Ouch, dammit, hold me by the neck, too, not just the hair," she growled painfully.

"Sorry, Mom," he said, putting his free hand around her cold neck.

"Where the hell is my body, anyway?" Liz asked, her eyes searching back and forth, even though she was facing one way and couldn't see in any other direction.

"Well," Kyle said as he was looking at the chest freezer next to the fridge. "You see, your body might be a little mangled because it was kind of a tight fit, so I kind of folded it a bit so it would fit. Then the police determined that you might have run off in the middle of the night and I never got a chance to dispose of you, what with the whole zombie plague and everything."

"So what? You're saying my body is no good? Then how am I able to talk to you," Liz asked, irritated.

"It must have to do with the dead coming back to life, Mom. They're in the street now, walking around outside as we speak," Kyle explained. "For some reason you can still think. I don't know, maybe others can, too. Tell you the truth; I never tried to strike up a conversation with any of them."

"So that means if the dead are walking and I'm dead then I can't feel pain anymore. Listen, Kyle, I forgive you for killing me, okay? But now you need to make things right again."

"What? How can I do that?"

"That's simple, dear. You have to find me another body because I don't want to be just a head for the rest of my undead life. As for why I can talk, I have no idea either," Liz said.

"Okay, Mom, I'll see what I can do. I have to tell you, in all honesty, that I've missed you these past three months. Even all your nagging," Kyle said as he walked out of the basement and into his room. "Hell, there's plenty of bodies outside for you. I guess we just need to take one and see if I can stick your head onto it."

He took the stairs to the first floor, and when he reached the front door of the house, he decided not to go outside just yet.

"What's wrong?" Liz asked as he held her head up so he could look her in the eye.

"Well, I'm a little scared. I don't want to go out there and you know, shop for you," he said sarcastically.

"Okay then, maybe it's not such a good idea for you to go out there. So how about we go look out my bedroom window, and when I see one I like, you can take one of your swords and go out there and fetch it for me," Liz suggested.

"Okay, that could work," he nodded and quickly ran upstairs to his mother's old bedroom, but before he ran into the room, he grabbed the sewing kit out of the hallway closet.

"We're obviously going to need this," he said, while holding his mother's head the entire time, sometimes carrying her like a football.

Setting the sewing kit on the night stand next to the bed, Kyle opened the curtains to see the entire street below. He set Liz's head down on a small stand in front of the window so she could see outside.

"So, Mom, take your pick, the whole world is now your smorgasbord," Kyle said, pointing outside.

"I don't know, none of them look a good fit for me," Liz said.

"How about that one?" Kyle asked and pointed to a middle-aged woman with short blonde hair and a large wound on her left side. As she walked, a thin rope of intestine dragged behind her like an empty dog leash.

"No, I don't think so. The breasts are too small on her, but I do like her butt," Liz commented.

"Okay, then, how about that one?" he suggested.

"No, no, no, I don't like the butt or the legs, but I do like her breasts," she said, rolling her eyes.

Kyle sighed, this was like going clothes shopping with her when he was younger. She could never make up her mind what to buy.

Kyle sighed. "Okay, Mom, how about this then. What if I take some of the zombies that you like and gather 'em all together. I can take what parts you like from each one and then see if I can stitch everything together for the perfect body. Any other way, you're just a head, and you'll end up staying that way," Kyle explained.

Liz nodded, agreeing with her son for the first time in a long time. With that settled, Kyle set her on the bed and he quickly went to the basement to go get one of his swords.

Downstairs, Kyle grabbed the sword that he used to kill his mother with, thinking back to that one gruesome night. Pushing it down further into his mind, he ran back upstairs to the first floor and then to the front door. Unlocking it and opening it slowly, he saw there weren't too many ghouls around the house at the moment.

Taking in a deep breath, he threw the door open and made sure it was closed behind him. He crept down the walkway quietly, not wanting to be discovered just yet. Outside, he looked around to see what his mother had liked and then he spotted the zombie with the big breasts.

Going after her like he was hunting wild game, he saw that the zombie was probably in her late teens or early twenties, with a lip ring on her bottom lip, and black hair and black nails. She looked like she had recently been changed, not looking that bad in the decaying department.

Running at full speed at her, Kyle threw up his arms, both hands holding the hilt of the sword firmly, and then chopped the head off the girl in one swipe, just like he did to his mother months ago.

The head stayed put a good ten seconds, the slice was so clean, but then it fell off to roll away from the body. Blood squirted out of the neck hole, and making sure not to get any on him, he took the body and dragged it to the front porch of the house. With the body on the front porch, he spotted the next zombie woman with the Jennifer Lopez butt that his mother liked. He was about to go get her when the other zombie's saw there was food walking around among them; namely Kyle.

Figuring this out, he quickly ran over to Big Butt, making sure to stay clear of the swiping hands as the zombies tried to get a piece of him.

As he approached Big Butt, she turned and Kyle saw that her entire face was torn off, muscles glistening in the sun, her cheek bones as white as clouds. Closing his eyes, he brought his sword down to swipe at her, and making sure not to miss, his aim was true, but not where he wanted it to go.

He ended up slicing the sword at a horizontal angle and it cut through the lower torso of Big Butt, separating upper and lower potions like a dissection. The upper half of the body stayed balanced precariously, which seemed to be for minutes, but Kyle had no time so he just pushed the upper half off and grabbed a leg with his free hand. When the upper half of the body fell to the ground, the bifurcated zombie began trying to pull itself across the lawn to get to the person who stole its legs.

Reaching the porch, Kyle decided to use the sword like a spear and he threw it at the nearest ghoul, knowing he had plenty more in the house. The sword impaled the ghoul in the chest, sticking out like the toothpick in a cheese cube on a plate of party appetizers.

Opening the front door, Kyle picked up the headless corpse and the lower legs of the other one and dragged them both inside the house as quick as possible before any of the other zombies got too close. With blood everywhere, soaking into the carpet in the foyer, Kyle sighed with relief now that the bodies were finally in the house. Kyle then turned around and locked the door behind him, making sure no more zombies could enter. No sooner did the door click shut then the ghouls began to bang on the door once more.

Moments later, after dragging both bloody corpses up the stairs, and retrieving another sword from his room, he finally made it to his mother's room and dropped the corpses onto the carpet.

"Let's make some magic," Kyle said, cracking his fingers.

"What the hell happened out there?" Liz asked. "I saw you get the one with the big boobs, but then you were so close to the house I couldn't see you anymore.

"I'm fine, Mom. I cut off a few heads, did a dance around the zombies, no biggy. Now let me get to work," Kyle said, grabbing his sword and getting ready to cut up the two corpses for parts.

First he cut off the lower half of Big Boobs so it would match up with the other one so they could be put together easily, like a jigsaw puzzle. Putting the upper and lower halves of the bodies on the bed, Kyle prepared by getting a lot of yarn and the big needles from the sewing basket.

"Wait, Kyle, I think I like the legs on the big boobed woman better, but the butt of the other. Can you sew them on too?" Liz asked.

"Fine, all right. Hey, wait a second, I thought you said you didn't like the legs on that one," Kyle said.

"A woman can change her mind, can't she?" Liz asked.

Shrugging, he then started cutting off the legs of the lower half that was on the bed. Throwing those away, he got the other legs, blood dripping off the ends, the pelvic bone now lying all alone on the floor.

"Now just relax, Mom, while I do this. You won't feel any pain 'cause you're dead," Kyle said, tapping his mother on the head.

First, Kyle began to sew the legs onto the butt, taking his time and making sure to do a double stitch so the legs would stay on.

"Okay, I have no idea how this will work or even if you'll be able to control these new legs of yours, but it might be okay," Kyle said as he finish the stitching on the left leg a few minutes later.

Ten more minutes passed and then he was finished with the other leg. He sat back and admired his handiwork, feeling very proud. Then he reached for Liz and worked her head onto the shoulders. He reached under the jagged flesh of her neck and began sewing the veins and nerves together. He didn't know what he was doing but figured if the dead could walk then what did he have to lose?

"Mom, try to move your new legs," Kyle said after finishing twenty minutes later.

After a few trials and errors, she finally got them to work, even though she had no idea how she could manage this.

"Great job, son, now finish the rest of my body, and be careful, I don't want that butt scratched," Liz joked.

Kyle nodded, pleased he was going to have his mother back. He'd been so alone these past few months that he hadn't realized just how much he loved her until she was gone and then back in his life again.

Sure, she could be a pain, but she was still his one and only mother.

Several hours later and after constant sewing, Kyle was finally done putting his mother together.

"Can you move your hands?" Kyle asked.

Trying, Liz finally was able to move her hands and then even her new arms. After a few minutes of testing out her new body, she decided to get up and try to walk around, like she was trying out a new pair of shoes.

"Wow, I can't believe you're finally doing it. I mean, even though I tried my best to stitch the nerves together I really didn't know what the hell I was doing. It still doesn't make any sense," Kyle said in awe of seeing his mother moving around.

"It doesn't have to make sense, dear, I'm dead. Now stop standing around with your hands in your pockets and start cleaning this place up, it's a mess. Then go cook your dinner, and if you don't do a good job, you'll be grounded for the rest of the apocalypse," Liz snapped, pointing to the things she wanted him to clean as she studied herself in the mirror mounted on a wooden stand near the side of the bed.

Rubbing his eyes together, Kyle sighed, now remembering why he'd killed her in the first place.

As he shook his head wearily, he reached over and picked up his sword. Liz noticed this and stopped admiring herself as she turned to glare at him, her mouth curled up in annoyance.

"Kyle, just what in the world do you think you're doing? I told you to get cleaning," Liz told him.

"Sorry, Mom, I tried," he said as he lifted the sword over his head and brought it down onto the top of his mother's head, slicing it in twain like a watermelon at a picnic.

With the blade firmly in the middle, the two parts of the head fell to each side like a scooped-out grapefruit to clatter onto the floor, brains sliding out to soak into the carpet.

"Oh, well," Kyle said, "back to the drawing board."

At least now he was finally free from his mother's rantings forever.

DOMENIC GIANGREGORIO

CARNIVAL MADNESS

"Welcome, welcome, one and all. To the best circus of your lives," said a clown while balancing himself on a large ball.

The crowd clapped with laughter.

Well, all except a boy who hated clowns.

He never laughed when he saw one. Didn't even smile.

"Now, for what you have all been waiting for. I will, no kidding, swallow a whole sword," the clown said as he jumped off the ball.

The clown grabbed a long sword from a table and then he took it out from its case.

"Well, here I go," the clown said while raising the sword into the air.

The audience was quiet, all watching with baited breath.

The sword entered the clown's mouth. The sword went down, and down, and down. But then the clown coughed up some blood. The crowd gasped. Even the boy. The clown went down on his knees and as the clown pulled the sword free, it dropped out and bounced onto the ground. From the tip of the sword to the beginning of the handle, it was covered in blood.

"I guess this is my final act folks. I hope you had fun," the clown said as he dropped to the floor in silence, his insides now chewed up from the sword.

The clown was dead and people began to cry as some screamed with fright.

"Look, Mommy," a little boy said to his mother. "The clown isn't dead!"

The mother looked and she gasped in shock. The clown was getting up.

The clown slouched as he walked towards the crowd. The boy who didn't like clowns looked at the clown as he slouched.

The clown's face looked hungry. Maybe even starving.

"Look out!" the boy yelled.

The boy who hated clowns pushed the other little boy out of the way. But he couldn't save the mother. The zombie clown grabbed the mother's neck and cracked it in two. Blood squirted out of her neck like a garden hose onto the floor. The boy who hated clowns looked at the zombie clown while holding the little boy in his hands.

"What's your name?" the little boy asked the older boy who had saved him.

"Rick. How about yours?" Rick asked.

"Nathan," the little boy said.

The zombie clown was still hungry. The mother had just been breakfast. The zombie clown walked slowly towards Rick and Nathan.

Rick looked around and found a shotgun on a nearby table that was supposed to be in the next act. Rick put Nathan down beside him and then loaded the shotgun with ammo and aimed it at the zombie clown.

"Take one more step and I'll shoot!" Rick warned.

The zombie clown lifted his foot and stepped forward. Rick shot the gun. The bullet went through the zombie clown's skull and out the back. Pink and red goo squirted out of the front and back of its head like a fire hydrant.

"Okay, eww," Rick said. "That's gross."

But the zombie clown didn't fall down, it kept on walking.

"I want my Mommy!" Nathan cried. "There she is!"

"What did you say?" Rick asked.

Nathan pointed up high.

Rick looked. "What is that?" Rick wondered.

Something was swinging down on a rope. Whatever it was its arm snapped in half and it fell into a pool of needles that were supposed to be for another act.

"Ouch, that must have hurt," Rick said.

"I'm guessing that was supposed to be for the find the *hay* in the *needle stack*," Rick said

Nathan laughed. The zombie clown moaned. That washed the smile right off of Nathan's face. What got out of the needle stack was Nathan's mommy.

When the zombie mommy climbed out of the needle stack a bucket of water fell on her. Some water went down and dripped into her mouth. Water was coming out of the zombie mommy's stomach as if a porcupine had attacked her, her torso now resembling a pin cushion.

"Mommy!" Nathan cried out again.

The zombie mommy walked towards Nathan. Her face looked hungry. The zombie clown followed her. Rick didn't know what to do. He looked down to his foot and saw a finger. The finger belonged to the zombie mommy. It had snapped off when she had landed in the needle stack.

Rick picked up the finger and put it in the muzzle of the shotgun. He aimed the shotgun at the zombie clown. Rick shot the gun. The zombie clown opened his mouth. The finger flew into the clown's mouth like a bullet as the rest of the blast hit him dead on.

"Wow. I guess that clown is a fan of lady fingers," Rick said.

But the clown was still coming, though half its head was missing. The zombie mommy was coming too and Rick didn't want to try and fight them any more.

Rick gave up and ran out through the front curtain with Nathan by his side. Nathan didn't want to leave his Mom but he listened to Rick.

They stopped in front of a red jeep parked near the entrance to the circus tent they had been in.

"Hey, dudes. Name's Bromly," a man said sitting in the driver's seat of the jeep. "If you want, you can come with me. I'll get you guys somewhere safe."

Rick and Nathan got into the jeep. After Bromly drove away the zombie clown and the zombie mommy came out of the circus tent.

As the jeep drove away, the two zombies began to follow, their steps slow but sure.

"Where're we going?" Rick asked.

"Wherever we end up, lad," Bromly said.

They ended up at a burger joint.

"I'm hungry," Rick said.

"Yeah, me too, but I still miss my mommy," Nathan said.

"Then let's go inside and get something to eat," Bromly said.

They went in and sat down at a table with red cushions.

"How can I help you?" the waitress asked.

"We'll just have the special," Rick said.

"Right on it," the waitress said.

Rick, Nathan and Bromly waited a couple of minutes and the waitress came back.

But instead of meatloaf, she brought back brains. They were red and pink and slid on the plate like large worms.

Rick looked at the brains and his face took on a green tint.

"I think I lost my appetite," Rick said.

"It's all we have," the waitress said with a shrug.

"Then were not eating here," Rick said. "There's a couple of zombies following us, they'll love the special here."

Rick, Nathan and Bromly left the joint and drove off into the sunset.

While they were driving, they came upon a warehouse.

"Gee, I wonder what's inside?" Rick said.

"Let's go check it out, there might be something good in there," Bromly said.

"Rick and Bromly left Nathan in the jeep and they went into the warehouse. The door was blocked on both sides but Bromly kicked it open with a good kick.

"Hello!" Rick called into the warehouse, but there was no answer.

Bromly heard sobbing coming from an old rusty metal cabinet in the corner of the warehouse. As Bromly went to investigate, Rick saw a computer disc on a dusty desk.

"Hmmm, this could be of some use to us," Rick said

Bromly opened the cabinet to see nothing but hanging uniforms and a few hangers, and when he peeked inside he saw no one. When he turned around, he saw Rick and he looked right at him.

"No one's in here," Bromly shrugged. "That's so weird I could have sworn I heard someone crying."

Rick, who could see Bromly clearly, who now had his back to the closet, didn't understand when Rick gasped in shock.

From behind the uniforms, hidden when Bromly checked, a zombie lunged out of the closet directly at Bromly's throat.

"What the!" Bromly screamed.

"Look out," Rick screamed to Bromly.

Bromly turned around and the zombie landed on his chest, both of them falling to the dirty floor

Rick grabbed a board with a nail in it that had been leaning against the back of the desk.

"Duck," Rick yelled as he swung the board.

Bromly ducked and the nail in the board went into the back of the zombie's head. Blood splattered all over Bromly's face and the zombie's head was whacked against a loose piece of wood that was sticking up in the floor.

But it was more than that. This entire section of floor was crumbling and old, and as the zombie landed on this part, the floor collapsed, the zombie disappearing in a cloud of dust.

A piece of wood was broken when the floor collapsed and it flew up and hit Bromly's head, causing a small cut.

The zombie fell down through the space in the middle of the floor. But no sooner did the body disappear then more hands were crawling up from the basement.

"There's a whole bunch more down there!" Rick screamed as he helped Bromly up.

"Let's get the hell out of here!" Bromly screamed in shock.

And that's what they did. Returning to the jeep, Nathan relieved to see them unhurt, they drove off into the setting sun, while behind them, in the warehouse, dozens of zombies began to crawl out of their basement prison, free at last to roam the Earth.

ANTHONY GIANGREGORIO

IT'LL ONLY HURT A LITTLE

The grunting grew louder as Clyde prepared to climax for the second time that night.

His hips grew tense and his face took on the look one gets when a particularly difficult shit was wracking one's body.

"Oh, God! Oh, yeah, here I come, baby!" he screamed as he felt himself release and he shot his load into the cold cavity of the dead girl's pussy.

"Oh, yeah," he breathed as he rolled to the edge of the crypt in the center of the mausoleum and sighed happily.

Next to him was the two month old corpse of a sixteen year old girl.

The girl's name had been Stephanie.

She had been hitchhiking one night when she'd gotten into the wrong car. The driver had sodomized her, beat her and just plain treated her like a pile of shit.

Stephanie hadn't survived that night, and the massive black and blue bruises covering her broken neck proved this. Even the mortician's makeup couldn't completely hide the marks.

Now, two months later, she was being abused again, this time by Clyde.

Clyde Milton worked in the Rosemont Cemetery, home of over thirty thousand graves. Loved ones from all walks of life were interred here, each mostly forgotten by the living.

Sure, cars would drop by on weekends and religious holidays, but for the most part Clyde had seen that once you died, people forgot about you. Not that he blamed them. You had to move forward or you'd be miserable all the time.

But Clyde didn't forget all those dead and buried people. Especially the women.

A few weeks ago a mother of about forty had died of a coronary. Clyde had waited for the funeral to end, and when he knew everyone was gone, he had opened the coffin and snuck the body to his old and beat-up van. The same one he carried the flowers and yard implements to keep the cemetery landscaped.

The Rosemont sign was painted on the side too, of course.

He'd brought the dead woman back to his small shack at the back of the cemetery and had ridden her for a week straight. Even when the smell had begun to get overwhelming, still he had ridden that fine, dead ass.

It was when he had the woman on her knees, holding her arms up so she wouldn't fall over that he knew it was time to put her back into the ground.

As he pumped her from behind, her right arm had begun to separate at the upper socket. First the flesh began to tear and then finally with a dull *pop*, the arm detached. Clyde had been about to cum and he'd been thrown off balance as both he and the woman tumbled to the dirt-covered wooden floor. She'd ended up on top of him and as he shot his load into the air, her face had come down on his, like she was kissing him, perhaps thanking him for such a lovely evening.

Clyde had screamed then, pushing her off him, thinking she had somehow come back alive and was now trying to get him for what he'd done to her. But as he tossed her away from him, the body merely flopped down, then lay still.

His penis had deflated like a shrunken balloon and he lay there on the floor panting, his heart feeling like it was going to burst from his chest.

After that little experience he didn't touch another corpse for three weeks, but soon the urge overcame him and he knew he couldn't resist.

Which worked out well because that was when Stephanie arrived. She had looked so sweet in the open casket, as the wake had been held in the main house.

Clyde had managed to sneak in, and he had grabbed a peek of the body.

The instant he saw those small pert cheeks, the budding bosom, the small nose, he knew he had to have her. As he left the house, his pants were pitching a tent something fierce and he had to do his best to hide it.

It had been a long day and a half and then he had to wait for the wake to end and then the next day the funeral too, but finally it came and went and he watched from the edge of the tree line as they mourned poor Stephanie and said their goodbyes.

Eventually it ended, everyone left, and Clyde knew that should be his cue to drop the casket into the hole with the winches and to fill it.

But as he stared down at the coffin, he knew he had other plans for the sweet thing within. He didn't even wait to get her back to his shack, but instead brought her to the nearest crypt.

Clyde had always been an odd bird.

When he was twelve and first found out about sex, he'd gotten the idea to see what it would feel like to fuck the neighbor's dog. But as he tried to wrestle the animal to the ground, his pants down around his ankles, he ended up snapping the dog's neck.

As he stared at the dead animal, his mind racing for what to do next, he came to the conclusion that what just happened might not be such a bad thing.

After all, the dog was still warm and now it couldn't fight him.

But later, when the dog had grown cold and he'd fucked it again; he found his orgasm was even better than the first time.

After that experience, Clyde found he had a natural attraction to dead things.

Having sex with a live woman was out of the question, what with their living eyes, breathing, and making noises.

Oh, no, he liked them quiet, not noisy as he pumped and pumped till he exploded.

Back in the present, Clyde rolled over and stared at Stephanie's dead face. The makeup from the mortician had sloughed a little, or maybe that was her skin. Her hair was still in great shape and her body was still soft. It would be weeks before she would begin to decay to the point he would have to get rid off her.

His right hand reached out and began to stroke her left breast. It was still soft, the nipple forever firm and perky. He could already feel his loins stirring and he leaned over and gently kissed the nipple, then wanting more, he began to suck it, caressing it with his tongue.

In no time he was hard again and he climbed on top of her, sliding himself back into her cold cavern. He liked it cold and wondered how any man could get off sticking his dick into a warm pussy.

As he stroked and pumped, he closed his eyes and imagined all the past fucks over the years. His breathing grew hard, and before he could stop it, wanting to enjoy every second, he felt himself exploding yet again.

Grunting in pleasure, he fell on top of the young, dead girl and sighed happily. Breathing in, her hair smelled like chemicals and to him it was the sweetest perfume. There was just the subtle hint of decay coming off her and to him it was the cherished ambrosia.

Climbing off her, he pulled up his pants, ignoring the bits of her still on the tip of his member. He'd clean it off later if he felt like it.

Picking her up in his arms, he left the crypt, tossed her in the back of his van and went home, happy as a pig in shit that had just gotten laid twice in one night.

The distance to his shack from the crypt wasn't far, and before he knew it he was pulling into the small, one car driveway.

Climbing out of the van, he skipped once in happiness at the thoughts of fucking young Stephanie later that night. He wanted to do her again now, but he wasn't as young as he once was and needed time to recover.

Cracking open the rear doors of the van, the moonlight seeped into the interior, casting Stephanie's face in a pallid glow.

For just a second it looked like she was staring at him, as if she was going to get up, and like a zombie from one of those horror movies, come at him, all gnashing teeth and clawing hands.

But then the shadows receded and he saw she was truly dead, just the way she was supposed to be.

Chuckling to himself at his silliness, he picked her up and tossed her over his shoulder like a slab of meat, her head and hands hanging down his back. She was butt naked and he couldn't resist squeezing her ass cheeks with his free hand, enjoying the way the flesh felt under his palm.

The door to the shack was unlocked as there was nothing inside worth taking.

Stepping through the doorway, Clyde's eyes rested on the heavy wooden table he used to eat on, and sometimes fuck corpses on.

Off to the left of the table in the small room were the sink, refrigerator and oven, and to the right was one door which led to a very small bedroom. Across the room was one last door which led to the bathroom, a two by four of a room with a sink, shower and toilet. Clyde always had to be careful when he sat on the throne or else he'd whack his head on the edge of the sink, it was that tight in there.

Clyde carried the dead girl to the table and laid her down, her head smacking the table.

"Ouch, sorry, doll, guess it didn't hurt too much, huh?" he chuckled as he went to the fridge to grab a beer, cracked it and took a pull, burping loudly.

That was when he realized he wasn't alone in his small shack and he spun around to see a tall black man wearing a crisp black suit with a white carnation on the lapel.

Clyde knew the man instantly. It was Mr. Rosemont, the head mortician, as well as the owner of the cemetery and mortuary. Both had been in his family for years and it was rumored the man, as did his father and grandfather, had a hand in the voodoo arts that went all the way back to his heritage from the dark pits of Africa.

Clyde thought it was all a load of shit, but the man paid his salary so he didn't give a fuck if the man knew God himself.

"Oh, shit, Mr. Rosemont, sir, ya scared me half ta death," Clyde said as he moved forward to shake the man's hand. He was so used to having dead corpses around him he didn't even think he should be concerned that he had just been caught with one in his shack.

Mr. Rosemont stared at the filthy hand like it was a snapping dog and would be an idiot to consider shaking it.

The man held an aura of power, his hair cut close to his scalp, his nails neatly manicured. This was a man whose family had crawled up from the gutter and he remembered where he came from.

Ignoring Clyde's proffered hand, he pointed at the dead girl on the table.

"You sick bastard, Clyde. I've been hearing rumors about what you've been doing to the bodies of the recently deceased but I couldn't believe it, so I decided to come here and talk to you about it. Out of respect of your years of loyal service to this cemetery I was hoping to get it all squared away. I told myself that no one could be so disturbed as to be fornicating with corpses, even you."

Clyde blinked at the man's words, realizing he was caught red handed. His mind racing, he knew what he needed to do immediately. He began to inch over to the small kitchen counter next to the oven while Mr. Rosemont followed, all the while talking.

"You'll go to jail for this, Clyde, you know that don't you? Do you know what they'll do to a pervert like you? Well, I don't want to even think about it. So you like to rape dead corpses do you? Well, I have a feeling when you get to prison, the shoe will be on the other foot."

Clyde reached the counter and his left hand crept around his back to grasp the handle of a cleaver resting on its surface. His other hand still held the beer and he took another pull, finishing half the can off in a few gulps.

"Now, Mr. Rosemont, be reasonable. I ain't hurtin' anyone. Shit, they're already dead. It's not like they know what I'm doin' to 'em."

Mr. Rosemont's eyes went wide as he took a step closer to Clyde.

"They don't know? But I do, dammit. People come here to put their loved ones to rest, not to have them desecrated by the likes of you. I'll see you pay for this with the maximum sentence allowable, Clyde. I have influence in this town. You're through, you hear me? Through!"

Clyde chuckled as his grip became so tight on the handle of the cleaver his knuckles turned white.

"Yeah, I hear ya, but it's you that's through."

Clyde brought the cleaver around and it sank into the side of Mr. Rosemont's neck, blood shooting out of the wound as soon as metal kissed flesh.

Mr. Rosemont stumbled away, his hand going to the cleaver embedded in his neck, and with shock filling in his eyes, he pulled the cleaver free.

More blood shot out, his carotid artery sliced in twain and the man stumbled to his knees, his breath coming in gasps.

"You...made a big mistake here, Clyde..." he gasped, his final moments on Earth drawing to a close. "Do you know who I am, what I can do?"

He fell to his knees and then to all fours as he grew weak from blood loss.

Clyde stepped closer to the fallen man and looked down, shaking his head.

"You mean that voodoo stuff? Shit, that's a load of bullshit and you know it, sir. You just let everyone believe that so you can keep people fearin' ya. Well, not me, I'm not afraid of no one."

"You will be," the dying man gasped.

Mr. Rosemont fell forward, his dark face now covered in blood. Clyde leaned over so he could watch the light leave the man's eyes. He was fascinated with death and he was already rubbing his crotch from the excitement of the kill.

Mr. Rosemont found the white carnation on his suit with a shaking hand and plucked it from his lapel. With his last gesture, he shoved the flower into his mouth and mumbled something so low Clyde could barley hear it.

"I will be avenged, Clyde, my death at your hands is only the beginning. You will pay..." he said around the carnation in his mouth. If he had more to say, it was lost when the man's eyes fluttered, then closed, his head sagging forward into the pool of blood on the floor.

Clyde snickered as he stared down at the man.

"Gonna make me pay, huh? Seems to me you're the one that paid, you nosy bastard. Shoulda just left me alone, shit, I wasn't hurtin' no one, the bitches are dead for Chrissakes."

Clyde stood up and walked to the doorway, where he opened it and stepped outside. He went to the van and hopped inside, then backed up the vehicle until the rear doors were facing his shack's front doorway.

He didn't feel like carrying the body anymore than he had to.

Walking back inside, he splashed through the blood and picked up the corpse of Mr. Rosemont, carrying it to the van where he tossed it inside without care. The body rolled over, the limbs flopping around and the once immaculate suit was now a mess. Mr. Rosemont's mouth opened and the carnation could be seen within. But where it was once white with a few spots of blood on it, the flower was now ebony black, as black as the darkest night or the deepest forest in Africa.

Clyde never noticed and he slammed the doors to the van closed, the matter of murder already forgotten.

With a smile on his lips he went back inside to have some more fun with Stephanie, now worked up after killing Mr. Rosemont. As he walked, he was already unbuckling his trousers.

He was so horny he thought he would burst; especially knowing that the young dead girl was waiting patiently for him to return to her.

As far as Mr. Rosemont was concerned, he could wait to be buried.

And buried he shall be for after all, Clyde lived in a cemetery, there were a hundred and one places he could bury the man where no one would ever find him.

But first a little fun.

An hour later, a few plot rows away from Clyde's shack, a fresh grave was being filled again. Clyde was sweating something fierce after digging the hole, but he wanted to get it done now before the next morning arrived.

There was a full moon high in the sky but despite this, the cemetery seemed as dark as the darkest night. It was as if the moon and stars didn't exist or that somehow their feeble glow was not reaching the cemetery below.

It was eerie, as if something not of this world was about this night.

But Clyde ignored the ominous feeling and patted the top of the grave, the loose dirt sliding off the mound just so.

Mr. Rosemont was four feet in the ground now. The man would never tell a soul what he'd discovered about Clyde. His dirty secret was still his alone.

As for Clyde, he tossed his shovels back into his van and headed back to the shack where the cool body of Stephanie still waited alone on the kitchen table.

As he drove through the cemetery, the moon waxing on the dull tombstones, he could already feel himself growing hard again in anticipation of what he was going to do to the girl's corpse.

Hours later, the moon now beginning its slow descent from the night sky as it prepared to vacate the horizon for another day, the darkness was complete.

The leaves in the trees of the cemetery fluttered as if on their own accord, the lack of a breeze disquieting. Nothing living was about this night, no crickets could be heard, no night birds called to one another. It was like the graveyard was truly dead, devoid of all life, mimicking the residents interred within its rod-iron gates.

On the fresh grave of Mr. Rosemont, the dirt began to shift, as if a rather large earthworm was working its way to the surface. This went on for almost an hour, but eventually the dirt parted and a black hand appeared, dark as night and blending into the surrounding gloom.

Eventually the hand became an arm, followed by another hand, then a head. To someone watching, if a living being had been in the cemetery this night, it would have seemed to be the stuff of nightmares, or low rated Z horror movies.

The earth shifted once more and Mr. Rosemont pulled himself free of his shallow grave, flopping onto the soil like a man pulling himself from the surf after almost drowning. His black, curly hair was filled with dirt and as he moved slightly the soil cascaded off his shoulders and hair to fall back onto the soft mound beneath him.

Dead eyes that somehow still could see gazed about the cemetery, *his* cemetery, and for a few moments the man's face was a blank slate. But then his right hand reached up and plucked the black carnation from inside his mouth, and with a moan, he set it back onto his lapel, the magical emblem filling his dead body with life.

Oh, yes, Mr. Rosemont had learned a lot from his daddy, and grandfather, to the point he never went anywhere without some sort of talisman.

And though he was dead, he would still get to exact his revenge on the person who killed him before being released into the oblivion of final death.

Standing on shaky legs, stiff with rigor mortis, his head slanted to one side, the bloody gash in his neck now filled with dirt, he raised his arms into the air and began to chant. The syllables were unknown to a civilized being, the words of the lost language handed down for so many years their true origin was lost in the folds of time.

But the words were powerful, containing mystic spells to bring the dead back to life. To breathe into the desiccated corpses buried around him a semblance of the life that had evaporated from their bodies upon their death like a puddle of water on a hot summer's day.

Where the man in black stood, slowly the graves around him and beyond began to tremble, as each corpse within the distance of his spell slowly stirred in their dark coffins. Soon, hundreds of graves were shaking as the bodies within fought their way back to the surface...to freedom.

Of course it would take time for them to reach the surface and many would never be free. Those who were placed in solid oak or metal coffins could never hope to break free of their cocoon-like prisons. But many were homeless people, indigents, who had been buried in simple pine boxes, others in body bags if the mortician thought he could get away with it, thereby saving a few more dollars off the already meager stipend the city gave him to inter bums and John Does.

These were the graves that began to vibrate as the bodies solely crawled to the surface and freedom. The older the corpse, the older the wood of their prison, thus allowing them to tear through into the wet soil above. Not needing to breathe, the dirt that might have suffocated them was ignored, and in time the first pale, skeletal hand began to push the moist earth to the side as the body slowly crawled into the cool air of a night of wonders, or a night of nightmares.

Hours later, more than a thousand zombies stood on rotting legs or crawled across the moist sod towards Mr. Rosemont. What was odd was they were all once men. No female corpses filled this army of the dead.

The mortician waited until all were close and then raised his arms high once more, moaning to the heavens. In turn, each ghoul with the ability to make speech in some form returned his gesture, and a thousand undead voices cracked with decay and filled with dirt, all wailed into the night sky. The sea of shifting heads seemed to undulate and sway as the massive crowd of dead folk waited patiently for their marching orders.

Satisfied, the zombie master smiled, the crease on his face looking like another gash similar to the one on his neck. Turning, he began moving towards the shack where he'd been murdered, to the shack where he would get his revenge.

And the man waiting within who would feel his vengeance in full.

Clyde was screwing the corpse of Stephanie again, his eyes creased in pleasure as he slid in and out of her cold hole. A jar of Vaseline was to his left, one he used quite often. The dead weren't slick down there and so unless he wanted to chafe, he had no choice but to add a little lubricant to the party.

His brow was sweaty and he grunted with each thrust, the dead girl below him shifting slightly. She was on her back, her eyes open, staring at the ceiling, and her mouth hung slack. She was like a mannequin made into flesh as Clyde abused her with each thrust of his body.

And then Clyde felt the moment coming, and with a yell of pleasure, he filled her with himself and then collapsed on top of her. His nose sucked in the scent of decay wafting off her and he could already feel himself growing hard yet again.

But his next bout of unnatural love was interrupted when the door to his shack began to shake in its frame.

"Now what the hell?" he mumbled as he crawled off the dead girl. "I don't know who's bangin' on my door this late but they're gonna get an ass whuppin'," he muttered as he climbed off Stephanie and began to get dressed. His penis was covered in Vaseline and a few bits of flesh, but he could have cared less.

Zipping up his pants, he picked up the cleaver, the same one he'd used on Mr. Rosemont, and went to the door to chase away the damn fool banging on his door.

Behind him, Stephanie lay still in death, her head now lolling to the side like a rag doll. Clyde reached the door, and with the cleaver held high to scare whoever was there, he opened it.

And promptly screamed with fear and shock.

Standing the in the doorway was a rotting man, complete with maggots squirming in his eye sockets. How the dead thing could see was anyone's guess, but as the door opened wide and Clyde shrieked, the zombie lurched forward to wrap its arms around his neck.

Clyde hadn't shrieked because of one lone zombie, he'd screamed because of the hundreds waiting behind this one, all in a similar state of decay.

But Clyde had been around dead people his entire adult life, hell, he had sex with them almost every day, and it didn't take him long to snap out of his fear induced stupor and deal with the zombie coming for him.

As the ghoul stepped into the shack, Clyde pushed it away from him and kicked the door closed, thus blocking the other ghouls from entry. Immediately, the door began to shake and the two windows of his shack imploded as undead hands reached inside for him.

With the cleaver held high still, Clyde swipe it at the ghoul's neck, the dry muscle parting like old parchment. The head bounced away to roll into a corner of the room, the mouth still blinking. But the body was still active and whatever had let it see without eyes still controlled it.

The zombie stepped towards Clyde, who with a snarl, slashed both hands off at the wrists.

The hands dropped to the floor where the fingers still grasped air, then the severed hands flipped over and scampered away like large, white spiders.

Clyde saw this but only out of the corner of his eyes as the zombie was still coming for him.

"Die you dead bastard!" he screamed and hacked at the body again and again, taking it apart piece by piece. Though the pieces still twitched, they were now harmless and he ignored them as he went to the windows and began slicing off hands at the wrists and then arms at the elbows. The limbs dropped to the floor like wilted roses off a bush after a big storm, where the hands then scampered away to be lost in the shadows of the shack.

As for Clyde, he was yelling and cutting, taking off each hand foolish enough to invade his domain.

Eventually, he realized there were far too many to stop on his own so he went to the corner of the shack and grabbed the old pieces of plywood, planks, nails and a hammer. With a snarl on his face, he ran back to the windows, and using the hammer to beat the hands away, he began to nail the wood over the window frames and then one across the door, just to be sure it was solid.

As he was hammering, he felt an itch on his leg, like if a mouse was crawling up his pants. When he glanced down, he saw one of the hands trying to climb up his pants and he whacked it with the hammer. But just as the hammer was about to connect, the hand dropped away and Clyde howled in pain as the hammer whacked his knee.

Muttering a thousand curses he began to limp as he searched for the damn hand so he could destroy it.

But there were more hands about, leftovers of his cutting rampage and they were lying in wait in the shadows of the shack.

Then the lights went out, one of the zombies outside pulling the electrical wires from the box out back of the shack and the entire room was thrown into darkness.

Clyde stood perfectly still, only the banging of the dead now piercing the inky blackness.

Then he moved to the small kitchen and found what he wanted, a small camping lantern he used when he needed to search for fresh bodies to fuck late at night.

The room was blasted with wan light as the lantern was lit and Clyde gasped when he saw more than two dozen hands surrounding him on the floor. If they had eyes it would have been like a herd of rats.

"You little bastards, I'll get ya for this!" he screamed and began running around the shack, stepping on the hands and smashing metacarpals to bits. When his foot left a pulverized hand behind, the fingers still twitched ineffectually, but they were done for.

He ran back and forth, knocking things over and grabbing the hands like he was an exterminator on the biggest job of his career. One hand got under his pant leg and he had to strip to get if off. When he was holding said hand, the fingers snapping back and forth like stubby snakes, he brought the hand to the kitchen sink, shoving it into the garbage disposal. It was an old model, found in the trash and installed by Clyde and it sounded like a locomotive was driving by, which was why Clyde rarely used it.

The disposal ground to life and Clyde smiled as he forced the hand into the circular opening. The hand seemed to scream in protest as it was slowly devoured into pulp, the bones finally jamming the disposal.

But the purpose was served and the hand was finished.

"Ha, I got another one of you bastards. I'll get you all and then I'll be safe. Your brethren can't get in here, these walls may look old, but they're strong as hell!"

The hands didn't reply and they scurried about, Clyde chasing them back and forth. One time when he tried to get one that had scurried under the sink and he inadvertently knocked Stephanie from the table. The corpse of the girl tumbled to the floor where she landed on her side.

Clyde ignored her and chased the hands, and as he went to one that had gotten behind the refrigerator, he was so preoccupied he didn't hear Stephanie as her body slowly started to twitch, then it got up and began crawl toward him.

Clyde was pushing the fridge out from the wall and using a broom handle to get the hand to leave the safety of the fridge, and he was oblivious to Stephanie's closing body.

With the moans of the dead and banging of fists on the shacks walls, the inside of the shack sounded like a rock concert crowd without the music.

So he never knew he was under attack until Stephanie used the hammer Clyde had set down and cracked him over the back of the head.

Clyde dropped like a steer with a bolt in its head and lay sprawled on the dirty wooden floor. As soon as he landed, the hands scurried out of their hiding places and hopped onto his body, some seeming to be sniffing the air with the tips of their fingers.

But Clyde wasn't out of it just yet, and as he stared at the hands over him and glazed up at the dead face of Stephanie--even in death she was beautiful-- he saw her smile, and as his bladder let go in terror at that grin, he fell into a darkness he assumed he would never awaken from.

But there were worst things than death and Clyde was about to find out one of them for himself.

As he lay unconscious on the floor, Stephanie went to the door with the hammer and pried off the wood to open it to the hundreds of waiting zombies.

As the door opened inward, Mr. Rosemont stood there, a tight grin on his face at the sight of Stephanie.

"Well done, my dear, soon you will have your revenge and your final rest," he said, his voice harsh now that half his neck was sliced. Turning, he gestured for a dozen zombies to enter the shack, which they did, one at a time or in trios. Three tried to enter the door at the same time and their shoulders became wedged, much like an old Three Stooges movies. The three decrepit ghouls were stuck, and though each pushed, their bodies were wedged in good. Mr. Rosemont sighed wearily and stepped up and grabbed two of the ghouls by the hair.

Yanking to free them, all he managed to do is pull the dry tufts free, scalp and all. With another weary sigh, he grabbed the middle one by the shoulders and yanked again, popping him free of his two buddies.

Now that the doorway was clear again, the ghouls swarmed inside. Mr. Rosemont directed a few to pick up Clyde and bring him to the table. The same one Stephanie had been abused on only minutes ago.

As the ghouls did as they were told, Mr. Rosemont smiled malevolently.

Soon Clyde would wake up and then the fun would begin, while outside the shack, a thousand zombies waited patiently for their next orders.

At first Clyde didn't know where he was and assumed he was in his small, filthy bed, but then he felt a hardness under his chest and stomach and realized he was lying face down on something hard.

On further inspection, he could feel his legs dangling off the edge, as if there was no weight on them, the hardness only pressing up to his groin.

And his head was at such an angle that it too seemed to be almost dangling off whatever he was on.

So he couldn't be on a floor, he reasoned.

Slowly he opened his eyes and no sooner did they open, then they snapped apart like small, spring traps.

He was still in his shack but he was now spread-eagled on his kitchen table.

And he was naked!

And it got worse. There was a room full of what were obviously zombies, as their state of decomposition would leave no denial. When he tried to turn his head and get up he found he couldn't.

Shifting his head as far as it would go, he saw he was being held down by five zombies. Also the severed hands he'd been trying to capture earlier were now on his back, their cold fingers pressing on his flesh, causing him to shiver.

But the zombies weren't moving, they all stood silently around him, a few moaning softly.

And then another shape came closer and Clyde was looking down at the now dirt-covered shoes of Mr. Rosemont.

"What the hell are you doing here? I killed you and buried you, you're dead! This has to be some kind of a dream."

"No, Clyde, it's no dream," Mr. Rosemont croaked. "You did kill me, but I was prepared for something like this to happen. You know of voodoo, black magic? Well, its real and so am I." He looked at the closest zombies. "As are my friends."

"Let me go, you bastard or so help me..."

"So help you what? What are you going to do exactly? Go to the police and explain that you killed your supervisor and then he came back from the dead. Or better yet, that you've been raping dead bodies for years and got caught? No, Clyde, even if you somehow escaped, which is unlikely, you won't be saying a word about this night. About any night ever again."

Clyde tried to pull his arms free, but the zombies held him fast.

"So then, what are you gonna do with me?"

Mr. Rosemont moved closer and leaned to the side so his face was less than an inch from Clyde's face.

Clyde winced at the smell, not used to fresh rot. The man was already decaying and Clyde realized the stench of pure rot was very different from when he got the bodies after they were embalmed. But he didn't show he was uncomfortable. He use to fuck dead dogs, he could handle the redolence of his former boss.

"When I get outta here I'll kill you again, dammit, and this time I'll make sure you can't get outta your hole."

"No, Clyde that won't be happening, for you see, I came back for a reason and that is to make you pay. For what you did to me and what you've been doing to the dead."

"Fuck you!" Clyde snapped.

"Oh, no, Clyde, not fuck me, it's fuck *you*," Mr. Rosemont said and then he nodded to the first zombie who was standing behind Clyde.

The ghoul moved up between Clyde's spread legs and positioned himself just so. Clyde's eyes went wide when he felt something moist and cold between his butt cheeks.

He felt terribly vulnerable being naked and for the first time since waking up he began to think he may have a problem here.

"What's going on back there, hey, cut the shit!" Clyde yelped to no avail.

Mr. Rosemont began to laugh as the zombie moved closer, positioned his stiff penis just right, and then slammed it in, Clyde screaming as he was penetrated like a virgin after her wedding.

"What the fuck? Get offa me, you asshole, goddammit!" he screamed as he felt himself being violated. But no sooner did he scream then another zombie was instructed to step up to his face, which was perfectly positioned at waist height. As he shrieked in pain at being violated from behind, the next zombie dropped trousers and shoved his shriveled, yet hard cock, into Clyde's mouth.

Clyde shook his head and before he knew it, he tore the penis off the ghoul. Stuck in his mouth, he used his tongue to force it out of his teeth where he then spit it out.

"You bastard, I'll see you die again, I'll get you!"

Mr. Rosemont shook his head as he motioned another zombie to move up to the man's face and then shove his stiff, yet desiccated penis into Clyde's mouth. Meanwhile from behind, the zombie had stepped back to allow another to take its place. This one had been a big black man in life and his member was the same and before Clyde knew it, he was being impaled like a spear had been shoved up his ass. The zombie began to pump as Clyde's muffled screams came out from around the zombie's dick pumping his mouth.

After a minute, Mr. Rosemont waved the large zombie away and let the next one in, who soon was slamming it home like it was no one's business. Clyde's anus was torn and stretched, the man bleeding internally, but still the next zombie came and began to pummel him like a fresh fish in prison.

"How does it feel, Clyde, hmmm? How does it feel to be violated the way you have done to so many of the dead? Like poor Stephanie here who had to lay there and take it. Now you can see how it feels."

Another penis broke off in his mouth and he began to gag, but then he was able to retch and the seven inch tool slid out of his mouth to bounce on the floor. One of the severed hands scooped it up and ran off, perhaps wanting a hand job.

Clyde sucked in a breath of agony as the next zombie slid between his legs and began to pump. Another zombie came to the front and shoved its maggot encrusted penis into his mouth, the steady rhythm as it pumped causing him to taste bile.

As the zombies continued to fuck Clyde to death, Mr. Rosemont glanced out the shack's doorway, at the long line of a thousand ghouls, which meandered through the cemetery, each waiting their turn to fuck Clyde in the ass and mouth.

With a slight chuckle, the mortician grinned, his white teeth a sharp contrast to his dark face, and he leaned down closer to Clyde's ear.

"I told you I'd make you pay for what you did to me, but don't you worry, Clyde, just try to enjoy it, just like Stephanie and the ones before her. There's only nine hundred or so zombies to go. In fact, if you close your eyes and try to relax, I bet it'll just hurt a little."

JOSEPH GIANGREGORIO

JUST DESERTS

Maria Groton thought she had the perfect life when she got married a few years ago.

She had a great secretarial job at a big firm in New York City, a huge house in the suburbs, a loving son, and she was in the best shape of her life.

There was only one thing wrong in her life, one bad choice that haunted her.

She had married a jackass.

Her husband's name was Tom Groton and Maria thought he was going to love her for the rest of her life and they would be together until death do them part, but she was absolutely wrong. Maria had been in a relationship with Tom for a total of six years, the marriage barely three years old.

She quickly found out she had fallen into an abusive relationship. She didn't want to get a divorce after only a few years of marriage or call the cops on him, or risk herself and her young son's well being.

Her son, Brandon, was the apple of her eye. He was just one month away from turning two years old and she couldn't remember the last time he didn't cry before bed, because almost every night Tom would slap and beat both Maria and then Brandon for something he supposedly thought they did wrong.

It could be anything. Whether it was because she forgot to take out the trash or she left a few dirty dishes in the sink, or Brandon left his toys on the floor, if Tom had an excuse he would beat them.

She was terrified he would lose control and actually kill Brandon one day. While he didn't pull his punches with her, at least he was gentler to Brandon, if you call a grown man beating a two-year-old being gentle.

Tom, in Maria's words, was a horrible and disgusting man. He used to be in great shape back when they'd first met, but he'd let himself go after getting married and that was when he began abusing Maria and later, when he was born, Brandon.

The hospital knew them well and though she always had to lie and say she fell down or hit her face on the edge of a door, she knew the nurses and doctors had more than an inkling of what was happening to her at home, but there was nothing they could do. Unless she filed a complaint, it was a domestic matter.

So, on this warm night of May, the night began like any other, with Tom coming home after a long day at work. There were many nights when he came home hours late, sometimes well after midnight.

To him, going out to the bars and cheating on his wife with hookers and strippers was no big deal. Tom had decided not to mess around this night and he arrived home at 7:30 p.m., and he wanted food and a beer and no back talk.

"Maria, where the hell is my dinner?" Tom demanded, as he walked through the foyer and into the kitchen.

"I'm sorry, Tom," Maria said. "I have the pasta boiling and garlic bread's in the oven. I spent all day straightening up the house. It's been cleaned to your liking, which is to say, I followed the instructions you left for me this morning. And please, Tom, don't swear around Brandon, I don't want him to turn out like you." She said this with a sour look on her face and knew she never wanted Brandon to be like Tom or treat any woman like he did to her.

"To hell with him. He's already heard a whole lot of curses since he was born. Trust me, babe, his virgin ears are out of here," Tom sneered as he sat down for dinner. "And I'm still waiting for my damn beer."

Maria realized she'd messed up. She was supposed to have a beer waiting for him when he walked through the door. Not wanting to anger him, she grabbed one from the fridge, got a glass, and set them on the table in front of him.

As Maria was about to open the oven door to take out the garlic bread, she paused when she heard Brandon crying in the other room.

"Oh, shoot, Brandon's crying. Tom, will you please do something for a change and take the bread out of the oven instead of just sitting on your butt," Maria stammered, and then she was rushing out of the kitchen to care for her son.

"Screw that kid. All he does is cry, wah wah wah, all goddamn day," Tom said, stomping his feet as he stood up from his chair and walked over to the refrigerator to grab another beer.

When he opened up the refrigerator door, he found to his surprise that there was no more beer.

"Hey, Maria, where the hell are all my Budweisers?" he screamed, trying to be heard over Brandon's cries.

"I'm sorry, I didn't get a chance to go to the store today and get your *precious* beer," she called from the next room, trying to calm down her son.

When she finished calming Brandon down, the fire alarm began to screech, and when she looked into the kitchen, she saw a small cloud of black smoke was pouring out of the oven.

"Tom, the garlic bread!" Maria yelled as she ran into the kitchen with Brandon in her arms. The alarm screeched louder, alerting everyone to get out of the house if this was an actual fire. Brandon started to cry again and she didn't want to put him down, but she needed to get that bread out of the oven.

"Screw this shit, I'm outta here," Tom said, throwing his arms in the air and stomping through the foyer on his way to the front door.

"Tom wait, please help me!" Maria called as she began to weep, her son held tightly in her arms.

"Take care of it yourself! I'm going to the bar and when I get home if my dinner isn't ready you're going to get the beating of a lifetime!" Tom yelled, as he slammed the front door behind him.

With Brandon crying and the fire alarm screeching, Maria slumped to the kitchen floor, her back leaning against one of the cabinets, left alone with Brandon crying in her arms.

It was all too much and she had an emotional breakdown as tears of pity and frustration flowed down her cheeks like two tiny rivers.

As Maria cried on the kitchen floor, outside, Tom made his way to his truck and the neighbors all began to emerge out of their houses to see what all the commotion was about.

As Tom climbed into his Dodge truck, seeing his neighbors on their front lawns, each one looking and pointing at him, he flicked every last one of them off and told them to, "get a life," and, "mind your own damn business."

As he slammed the driver's door closed, he slid the key into the ignition and raced off down the street on screeching tires, leaving his screw-up for a wife and brat for a kid in the rearview mirror.

He wondered if she'd have his dinner ready when he got back, and though he knew he'd be hungry; at the same time at least he'd have an excuse to slap her around if she didn't. But then again, maybe he didn't need an excuse. Maybe he'd just return home and slap her around for the simple fun of it.

After all, there was no one to stop him.

Traffic was light, rush hour now over, and it didn't take him long to reach his favorite strip club in the middle of the city, but beforehand, he had to stop by an ATM machine and get some cash to put in the stripper's g-strings.

It took less than a minute to grab his money and get back on the road, and a few minutes later he pulled into a parking space for the Diamond Horse Club.

Before leaving his truck, he paused and took off his wedding ring, wanting to show the ladies he was available. With that done, he turned off the ignition, climbed out of the truck, and then strutted his stuff as he walked through the front door of the club, paying the cover charge with a grin.

The first thing he saw were five stripping tables on the left and each of them had a perfectly shaped woman gyrating on them, their forms ranging from blondes too brunettes and white to black. He didn't really care what color they were, as long as they had big, soft breasts. To the right of him was the bar with a sexy waitress hastily giving a bartender her orders, and even though she was wearing a tight-skinned shirt that covered everything, you could still see her nipples poking through. She was also wearing skimpy short-shorts that showed off her fine legs and tight ass. As he came here often, he knew her name and so did she his.

Looking around, he decided to go and grab a beer before picking a table.

"Hey, Becky, how's everything tonight?" Tom asked as he reached the bar.

"It's going great, Tom. You want the usual?" she responded.

Tom nodded and Becky leaned over the counter, grabbed a glass and filled it up with ice cold beer from the tap.

As she handed it to him, Tom quickly took a sip and then turned around to see the landscape of the crowd; wanting to see if there was anybody worth hitting on. This strip club was slightly higher end and there were many female customers scattered throughout the crowd.

As he took another sip from his beer and shifted his eyes to the back of the club, to his pleasant surprise he spotted a young woman who appeared to be in her early twenties. As she turned to look at him, their eyes met from across the gloom of the club and she responded with a smile and the fluttering of dazzling blue eyes.

Tom took a huge gulp from his beer, finished off half the glass, then set it down on the bar and moved through the crowd.

It was as he was weaving through the partiers that he glanced down at himself and realized he was still in his work clothes. But then he thought to himself, *Screw it, all girls love working men.* Or so he thought.

When the woman saw Tom moving towards her, she quickly finished off the rest of her mixed drink, adjusted her bra and fixed her hair, so she would look suitable for the handsome man that was coming towards her.

Tom was licking his lips as he strode through the club, thinking how he might be getting some action in his truck tonight if he played his cards right. When he reached her, he quickly introduced himself.

"Hey, I'm Tom, what's your name, beautiful?" he asked, trying to be heard over the bass of the music.

"Hello there, Tom, I'm Alexis. Are you from around here?" she asked, wanting to get to know him.

As she introduced herself to him, he took the time to study her features. The thing that caught his eyes the most was her two large breasts that looked to be double D's and he couldn't take his eyes off of them for second. The shirt she wore was open in front and the long line of cleavage where the two glorious mounds touched was driving him crazy. All he wanted to do was stick his face in there and rub it around.

But there was more to see. He shifted his gaze to her legs and saw they were perfect, like they were carved out of stone by a master sculptor. There was not one imperfection or blemish on them. Realizing he took a little too long admiring her, he finally spoke up and looked into her beautiful blue eyes.

"Yeah, I live just outside the city. And how 'bout you? Why would such a beautiful woman like yourself be caught dead in a strip club?"

"Well, I'm new to the city and I don't mind watching hot woman showing their stuff and this is also a good spot as any to pick up guys," she said. "Was I correct in that assumption?" She batted her eyes at him seductively.

Holy shit, this girl loves going to strip clubs and she's a bombshell, she's the total goddamn package, he thought.

To say he loved women with huge and supple breasts was an understatement for him because everywhere he went, it seemed he spotted women with big tits.

Well, except for the woman he had at home. Maria's breasts were small and perky and he could cover them easily with his hands. They were nice but they didn't get his engine revving.

He then decided he wanted this woman badly, but he didn't feel like playing games with her or risking getting shot down, so he took a chance and decided to go in for the kill and close the deal.

"Listen, Alexis, I don't want to play games with you, all right? You don't strike me as that type of woman so I tell you what. I'll give you five hundred bucks in cash if you'll give me a blow-job in my truck." As he said this he pulled the money out of his pocket.

She never paused to consider the offer, but just nodded her head with a grin.

"Sure, I've haven't given one in a while and to top it off, I think you're gorgeous, and I always love men with a little sweat on their brow."

Great, he thought, immediately. *I wonder if I could've gotten her to do it for a hundred or two.* Then he shrugged. *Okay, she must be really stupid or really drunk, but all in all, a blow-job is a blow-job.*

"Okay, great, then let's go," he said, pulling her by the hand through the club and outside to his truck.

Ten minutes later, Tom was making sweet love to his newly acquired partner behind a condemned building a block away from the club. He was most defiantly getting his money's worth as the initial blow-job had lead to even more fun.

As the two people were locked in a lover's embrace, the truck rocked back and forth in the shadows of the empty alleyway.

They were both moaning and groaning as if they were one voice, the two of them both having orgasms at the same time. With a grunt of pleasure, Tom felt himself explode inside her and he buried his face in her breasts. Alexis felt him climaxing and she quickly climbed off, not wanting to get pregnant and realizing he wasn't wearing the condom he'd said he was going to put on.

"Dammit, Tom, you said you were gonna wear a condom. Why the hell didn't you warn me before you were gonna do that, you bastard," Alexis said as she climbed off of him and into the passenger seat. "What if you got something? You might have Herpes or Christ, even Aids. What the hell were you thinking?"

"Yeah, yeah, so sue me. I'm clean, relax. I should worry about you. A woman who'll give a guy a blowjob and a screw just like that must have something. But I like to live on the edge, baby, that's me. Now finish cleaning up and get dressed on your own time. Get the hell out of my truck," Tom said with a sadistic grin.

"What! You're not going to drive me home? But I have no way of getting back to my condo and..." She stopped and noticed the wedding ring on the dashboard for the first time and questioned him about it.

"Is that a wedding ring? You bastard, you fuckin' cheated on your wife? That's awful," she said as she stepped out of the truck half-naked, still trying to put her clothes back on. "You're some piece of work. I thought you were a nice guy, too."

"Huh, I'm a sweetheart, honey. You just have to get to know me better."

"No thank you. Now where's my money," she said waiting for him to hand it to her. "I'll take a cab, then."

As he turned on the ignition, he reached over and tossed a twenty out to the ground, and closed the door on her, slamming the door locks home. She reached for the handle and was slightly surprised to see the door was now locked.

"Hey, what gives, open the damn door, Tom!"

"I don't think so, babe. That wasn't so great after all! Be glad I left you the twenty!"

He backed his truck out of the lot and right into oncoming traffic while everybody around him on the street started blazing their horns as he cut them off.

"You asshole, I hope you get what's coming to you!" Alexis screamed at the receding truck as she gripped the twenty in her hand, waving her fist in the air in anger. Then she saw a cab and flagged it down, the cab driver looking at her with wide eyes as this half-naked woman climbed into his backseat. She told him to mind his own business and keep his eyes facing front, then she gave him her address. Without another word he drove off.

Oh, well, at least the twenty would get her home.

Three streets over already, Tom glanced down at the clock on the dashboard, the glowing numbers reading 12:30 a.m.

It was time to go home.

He'd given Maria plenty of time to get his dinner ready, and after the sex he'd just had he was starving. If she was smart, she would be waiting in the kitchen for him.

The red stop light he was at took forever to change, and when it did, he took a right. Before he was fully through the intersection, he glanced to his right to see a yellow cab driving past him. In the back seat was Alexis, and she was still struggling to get dressed in the small confines of the vehicle.

As he drove home, his stomach growling for food, he grinned widely about getting *some* for free.

* * *

Still drunk, Tom swung his truck into the driveway of his house and found that his wife wasn't inside with dinner waiting, but instead she was sitting on their front stairs with a suitcase beside her.

In her arms was Brandon, the boy sleeping softly.

Tom turned off the truck and climbed out, his shoes slapping the pavement, and as he stared at his wife, the suitcase broadcast her plans to him in volumes.

"What the hell's this? Why aren't you inside of that house with my damn dinner? Shit, I gave you enough time. I've been gone for hours." He gestured to the suitcase. "And what's that for, you planning on going somewhere?"

"I would think that's obvious even to you in your present state," Maria said. "I'm leaving you, Tom. I can't take this anymore. So I called my father and he'll be here in a few minutes to get me," she said, sobbing, Brandon stirring fitfully in her arms.

"Are you doing this because you're trying to get back at me?" Tom asked, his anger flooding to the surface. He was about to explode when he realized he was outside, where the neighbors would hear. Well past midnight, only the soft sound of crickets could be heard and an occasional car passing by at the intersection at the end of the street.

But then he began thinking a little more, trying to smooth this out and maybe get her to come to her senses.

"Okay, listen," Tom said with his hands held out in a *slow down* gesture. "How about we talk this out like adults inside where the neighbors won't hear us," Tom reasoned as he stepped closer to her.

"No, Tom, it's over. I just told you I'm leaving," she said, a fire now in her eyes, one he'd never seen before.

His mind raced as she stared defiantly up at him.

How dare she? How dare she talk back to him? He was the man in this relationship. He clothed her, fed her, put a roof over her head and this was how she repaid him? Well, there was no way in

Hell he was going to let her get away with this kind of disrespect. No way was she going to make him look the fool.

That was when the anger overwhelmed him and he saw red. Tom suddenly lost it and ran the few feet separating them, completely taking her off guard, and gave her a backhand across her face, the blow so hard it made her teeth rattle.

Before Maria realized what was happening, she was falling to the cement stairs with nobody to catch her, white light invading her vision like fireworks before she succumbed to darkness.

When her head struck the bottom step of the porch where a two inch rusty nail was protruding, the side of her skull impacted with a meaty *thwack*, the nail sliding into her skull and rupturing an artery. At the same time Brandon slipped from her arms to hit his forehead on the cement walkway, his small head not taking the blow very well. Brandon landed hard and he began to twitch and spasm, but no sooner did he start then the small boy became immobile, a thin rivulet of blood slipping out of the corner of his mouth and nose.

Maria was doing much the same, her body twitching like small volts of electricity were jumping through her body. She wasn't dead yet, but would end up in a coma if she was lucky, or if she was unlucky and didn't get medical treatment promptly, she would die.

Tom stood like a statue, staring down at the small form of his son and his unconscious wife and he slowly came to his senses, realizing what he'd just done.

He leaned over and touched the side of his son's neck, not feeling a pulse, and then he shifted to his wife, who still had a pulse, but it was so shallow as to be non-existent.

Damn it, he'd killed his son and his wife was hurt badly, and if she recovered she would tell the police what he'd done.

He knew this was more than a minor problem and that he had to put everything into perspective quickly or he would find himself in a jail cell with a new wife called Bubba who would defiantly be in charge of the relationship.

But if Maria was dead too and was gone, then she could never tell a soul what happened this night.

Looking down at the two bodies, he was filled with an overwhelming urge to cover his tracks; to make sure what he'd done wouldn't be discovered. Panic began to fill him, but he pushed it down, knowing if he lost it now then all was over before it began.

Looking around him, he let out a sigh of relief to see none of his neighbors were watching from lighted windows. All the other houses were dark; no one had seen what he'd done.

He decided he better get the body of his wife and his son out of the open before his luck ran out and that was when he remembered the shovel that was in the back of his truck.

Knowing what he had to do if he wanted to stay a free man; he picked up the cooling body of his son and carried it to the back of his truck. Tom then ran back to the still form of Maria, who was bleeding everywhere from her head wound and he knew he'd have to finish the job to make sure she couldn't talk...ever.

Picking up her body and throwing her over his shoulder, he ran to his truck and tossed her into the bed alongside his still son like she was nothing more than a sack of potatoes. The body rolled to the side with one arm coming up over her head like she was stretching, and her right eye opened a little, as if she was dazed or drunk and trying to stay awake.

Ignoring her face and the eye that stared at him, he pulled an oily tarp from the side of the truck bed and covered the bodies with it, tossing the shovel on top and using a few miscellaneous items to keep the ends of the material from wanting to blow around when he drove away.

It wouldn't do to have a side pop up at the same time a police cruiser pulled up behind him.

He could just imagine him trying to get out of that one.

"Oh, no, officer, I'm fine, thank you. I just killed my wife and son in a fit of rage and now I'm off to bury them."

With the bodies covered, he ran back to the front porch and grabbed handfuls of dirt from the flower garden to cover the blood from Maria's head wound, the dirt soaking up the plasma and making a dark slurry. It wasn't perfect, but as it was night and the moon wasn't full, it would do the job until the next morning when he could hose down the steps under the guise of watering his lawn.

Remembering what Maria had said about her father picking her up, he grabbed her suitcase and tossed it into the rear bed too, and by doing this hiding all evidence of what she had planned tonight.

Then he ran into the house and wrote a quick note on a piece of paper, then taped it to the front door.

Making sure all the lights were off, he locked the front door and stepped away to inspect the front of his house.

Nodding, pleased with himself, he was confident things looked normal. The note on the door told his father-in-law to go home, that Maria and him had worked things out and that she would call him in the morning. Of course, she never would, but later he would tell him and others who asked that she had taken off in the middle of the night with his son; and this after they had reconciled.

It was perfect.

He dashed back to his truck, and as he climbed into the driver's seat, he saw a set of headlights coming down the street

Moving fast before the vehicle could get too close, thinking that this particular car might belong to his father-in-law; he quickly started the engine and drove off the other way, making sure not to turn on his headlights until he'd turned the next corner.

As he drove, his mind raced once again on what to do with the two bodies and then it came to him, the most natural place in the world was only a mile or so away.

The cemetery, of course. After all, that's where you put dead people and he had two more tenants in the back of his truck.

Feeling good about his plan, he headed off down the road, actually beginning to feel better, knowing he was going to get away with it.

A short time later, Tom arrived at the cemetery. Now that he was able to process what had happened, he began to rationalize his actions, as if by spinning it, he could make himself feel entirely guilt free.

By the time he reached the gates for cemetery, he'd decided both Maria and Brandon were just huge leaches that had been sucking the blood out of him and it was good that he'd gotten rid of them once and for all.

It looked to him like he didn't really want to settle down after all.

The metal sign welded to the seven foot, iron rod fence had the words **Newland Cemetery** etched in gold plating.

The gates were open, but then they usually were. Sometimes vandals would come in and mess around; knocking over a few tombstones, but for the most part the cemetery was left alone. So the gates could stay open all the time, and that way anyone could visit a dead relative whenever they felt like it.

The Dodge truck drove through the opening, the wide body of the rear bed threatening to scrape against the gates posts, but then he was inside without a scratch to the finish.

A low fog hung over the low cut lawn about a foot high and it gave the place an old, horror movie feel. Tom ignored this, knowing this was real life and no matter how spooky the cemetery may feel, the only real threat he needed to worry about was from other humans, such as the police if they found him with two bodies in the back of his truck.

As he drove down the small roads of the cemetery, his eyes searched the shadows for an open grave, preferably one that would be used tomorrow or the next day. His plan was to dig the grave a little deeper and then toss his wife and son into the hole. Then, at the scheduled funeral the next day, the coffin of some asshole would be dropped on top of the two bodies and no one would ever no there were two more guests interred.

It was so simple it was perfect.

Off to his right, he could see the mortuary, where they prepared the bodies for the funeral. The basement was where most of the work was done and he could see there were still lights on. Someone was working hard getting some stiff ready for their day of the dead, he figured.

A few more minutes went by, Tom making his way through the cemetery until he was deep inside the even-rowed lanes, and then he finally found what he was looking for.

As he turned onto the grass-covered earth and off the gravel road, he found the standard hole that was supposed to be for a loved one. He checked around and saw no one around, and feeling confident he was fine, he grabbed the shovel, his deceased wife, and his son from the bed of the truck, and then half-carried and half-dragged each of them to the grave in which they would be laid to rest.

He had to chuckle a little at the thought of burying them in this particular cemetery for free. His mother was buried here somewhere and it had cost a small fortune to put her here a few years ago, the plot alone a pricey item. He'd felt the cemetery owners had gouged him good, but it's not like he had a choice, so he'd forked over the money.

Now, he was planting his wife and son for free, and screwing the cemetery out of the business at the same time.

The truck's headlights were his only source of light for him and he quickly doused them, not wanting anyone to see him. With the headlights on he could be seen easily by a caretaker or perhaps the cops. He didn't actually know if the latter drove through the cemetery, but it would make sense as they would be patrolling for vandals or young lovers looking for a secluded place to park and fool around.

It took a second for his eyes to adjust to the night, but once they had he could see fairly well. There was a half moon out and the clouds were few so the stars were able to add their feeble glow to the dull gloom.

Jumping down into the open grave, he began digging into the bottom soil with his shovel. He worked fast, scooping out dirt and tossing it onto the edge. He figured three feet should do the job nicely as he sent the dirt up into the air to land on the lawn.

When he was finished, his body coated with a sheen of perspiration, he reached up to climb out and for a few seconds felt a paralyzing fear when, as he grabbed the edge, the earth crumbled under his fingers.

Jumping higher, the same thing happened again and he realized he may have literally dug himself into a hole. What a way to be found in the morning, him stuck in the hole and the bodies of his wife and son on the grass above him. But in desperation he tried again, and this time he jumped high enough to get his hands onto the grass, the sod just strong enough to let him pull his body up and over the lip. He rolled over and gasped for air as he stared at the night sky, then he got to his knees and shoved each body into the now deeper grave, a dull thump floating up as each corpse landed heavily, though Brandon's was much softer.

Standing up, breathing heavily from his exertion, he gazed down at what was left of his family. The family he'd inadvertently killed.

He almost felt some guilt rising up inside him, but he pushed it back down, not wanting to let it get to him.

He looked down on Maria's face, her eyes open as she struggled to suck in one last breath of air. Even if she wasn't about to be buried, she was on the verge of death anyway.

He pointed at her accusingly. "This is your own damn fault, Maria. All you had to do is listen to me. Was that so damn hard? If you didn't try to leave me then you and Brandon would be home right now, not lying in a damn hole. You stupid bitch." Spittle was flying from his mouth now as he tried not to let his guilt consume him. Each time it threatened to, he'd push it back down.

Looking around the dark and gloomy cemetery, he decided he'd been here long enough and should finish up before he was discovered, so he started to shovel dirt into the grave. As he did this, he thought he caught the scent of decayed meat on the air, but figured it was just his imagination running away from him.

After all, he was burying corpses in the middle of the night in a cemetery, how's that for a horror movie?

A few minutes later, Maria and her son were buried under a foot of soil and Maria breathed her last as dirt clogged her airway and she suffocated. Her only mercy was she never regained consciousness from the blow to the head and so drifted off into death painlessly.

As Tom shoveled the last scoop of dirt into the grave, he began hearing moans and groans on the wind, followed by the crackling of leaves and twigs, as if feet were crushing the deadfall littering the cemetery grass. It was a scuffling, shuffling sound and he couldn't put his finger on it as to what it might be. His mind conjured images of monsters and he felt a chill slide down his spine.

He was so preoccupied with the noises; he let the shovel slip from his fingers to fall into the grave. It clattered to the bottom where it lay still and he wanted to get it but then more noises came to his ears, so he decided to leave it.

It was definitely time to leave this place.

His earlier drunkenness was long gone and he was painfully sober as adrenalin filled his system. Fear touched the back of his mind and caused his stomach to turn within him.

With one last look at the soon to be hidden grave of his wife and son, he sprinted back to his truck.

Reaching the Dodge, he opened the driver's door and was about to climb inside when he felt something clamp around each of his ankles. With a yank, something pulled him off his feet and then he was tumbling to the ground. He landed heavily, not able to brace his fall and the air left his chest in a *whoosh* of expelled air. As he lay on the grass, staring up at the night sky, he tried to shake the cobwebs out of his head.

That was when he felt something on his lower legs again. It felt like it could be a rat or a cat, maybe, the small sensation of legs or paws on him, but when he glanced down his body to see his feet, he let out a gasp of shock.

Though impossible, he saw the upper half of a deceased person crawling across the ground from under his truck, the dry entrails sagging behind and stretched out in the grass like loose rope strands. The face was like dried leather, the bone protruding through in some places, and as he stared in horror, a few choice, white and brown maggots slid out of the, eyes, ears and nose holes of the creature. The stench of decayed meat was stronger now and it washed over him like the dead air from a swamp, the same smell of rotting vegetation coming to mind. The corpse had no eyes, only gaping holes.

"What the hell? This can't be. No...no, get back, you're not real!" Tom screamed, scared of the thing that was attacking him as he tried to kick his feet and push the putrid face away. The mouth was hanging open and the brown teeth could be seen within, the withered tongue now more like a dried slug as maggots squirmed within, the tongue looking like another worm to the babies.

While Tom was struggling with his attacker, more and more ghouls were popping up from the graves all around him and the ghoul that still held onto him wouldn't let up. As Tom watched, the ground exploded with dirt as bodies crawled into the night air. Most were nothing but desiccated skeletons, though a few looked freshly interred, only the dirt and mud on the faces and attire giving this away. More than one had lips sewn shut and these ghouls opened their mouths, ripping the dried flesh, their sutures tearing the skin. Low moans escaped lips that should have never spoken again.

Tom screamed and realized he needed to escape fast or there would be too many to fight, so he kicked the ghoul that was holding his ankles with the heel of his foot, right in its nose, or the place the nose would have been if it hadn't rotted off years ago.

When he moved his foot away, he saw that section of the face was now caved in and maggots and night crawlers began to pour out of the jagged orifice.

But he was free and he rolled to his side, then pulled himself to his feet using the side of his truck.

He saw that he was being surrounded on all sides and the only safe way out of his predicament was over his truck. He then turned, ready to crawl onto the hood, then the roof and then into the rear bed of the truck, hoping to find a weapon or something to save his butt. But no sooner did he try this then another ghoul stumbled out of the darkness and wrapped its arms around him.

The scent of decay was overwhelming and he fought not to vomit as he bent at the waist and sent the ghoul flying over his shoulders. The ghoul hit the grille of his truck and shattered into a dozen pieces, the frail body not able to take the impact.

"Ha, you bastards aren't so tough!" he called out. "Bring it on! I'll take you all down!"

Another came at him from his right and he punched it in the face, his hand sliding in to the wrist as the brittle cranium collapsed under the blow. Shaking his hand of brain slime, he turned and kicked another in the groin, breaking its hip as it fell to the lawn. He brought up his foot and slammed it down on the fallen ghoul's head, pulping it like a rotten apple.

Spinning, he turned to face his next adversary, but instead of seeing a rotting pile of skin and bones, he stopped in shock when he gazed upon the dirt-covered body of Maria and Brandon.

Behind them was the open grave and Tom could see the wooden tip of the shovel he'd dropped into the hole now poking up in a corner. It looked like Maria had used the shovel as a ladder to pull herself and Brandon out of their shallow grave.

"It can't be. You can't be alive! I killed and buried you! I killed and buried you both!" Tom cried, too shocked to move or say anything else, as the person that he had a love/hate relationship with for years was now standing in front of him.

But as he stared in utter astonishment, he could see it wasn't really her, or it wasn't the woman he'd known.

Her hair was now matted with soil and every crevice in her face and clothing was also covered with dirt. Already a few choice insects had found her flesh enticing and had begun crawling around her face and neck, flies hovering near the congealed blood on her scalp where the dirt had become stuck, making a dark, black paste. Next to her, holding her left hand, was Brandon, the boy's face now covered in dirt and grime too. There was a large dent on the side of his small head where his skull had connected with the cement walkway. Congealed blood seeped from the boy's nostrils and out of the side of his mouth, and his dead eyes looked at his father accusingly.

Tom shook his head, not able to believe his own eyes.

"No, you're dead! I killed you! You're both dead!"

Maria then raised her right arm slowly, her index finger pointing at him. Her mouth opened and closed but no sound emerged. How could there? She was dead. Her lungs didn't take in oxygen anymore and her heart didn't beat.

Tom, his eyes wide with fear, took a step backwards, preparing to run away, but as he turned to dash for his truck, he ran right into the waiting arms of more than a dozen ghouls, each one in a similar state of decay.

Every single zombie around him grabbed him, but Tom was having none it and he kicked the one's closet to him, breaking free of their feeble grip.

As he rounded the truck, he grabbed an umbrella lying in the rear bed, and deciding it was better than nothing, he used it like a sword, stabbing at the first ghoul to come for him. The tip of the umbrella punctured a hole through a ghoul's left eye and then went straight through and popped out the rear of the brittle skull. Dark brown and black brain matter began to pour out of the hole to splatter at the feet of the approaching ghouls. As Tom pulled the umbrella out, he then saw another zombie out of the corner of his eye that was trying to grab him, but he spun around and stabbed this one too, quickly knocking it down.

But he wasn't through and he ran to the fallen ghoul and started beating the head into mush; brains and dried, dust-like blood flying everywhere.

"This is what I'm going to do to all of you!" Tom screamed. "You can't beat me! You're all weak, and I'm strong!"

Swinging around to take down another ghoul, with more right behind it, he saw over the zombies' shoulders yet more animated corpse's crawling out of their graves, joining their brethren in the fight to kill him.

Deciding it was a losing proposition; he threw the umbrella at the closet zombie and started running in the opposite direction. He didn't care about his truck or that he could have gotten in and driven away.

Now only fear ruled his mind and all he wanted to do was escape this nightmare.

But as Tom trying to escape death at the hands of the ghouls, and the shadows of the night permeated every corner, he was oblivious to what was in front of him, the ground wreathed in darkness and fog.

It was while he was running away, already a few plots over from his truck, and the feeling of freedom was just beginning to grow inside him, that he felt the ground disappear under his feet.

He was falling and he cried out, but no sooner was he weightless then he landed heavily, dropping to his butt, not prepared for the unexpected landing. Looking upwards at the night sky, he found himself in an open grave, similar to the one he'd used for Maria and Brandon.

More than a score of zombies were now approaching the grave, some crawling while others shambled, and down below, Tom was desperately trying to escape, his fingernails literally being pulled out from scratching at the sides of the grave as he struggled to get free. But the grave was deeper than Maria's and he couldn't reach the edge by just jumping.

He stopped trying to climb out when multiple shadows crossed over the grave opening and he looked up into the pale and rotting faces that were surrounding him.

But they didn't try to get him; they just surrounded the grave, not moving, watching him like statues.

"So, come on, you dead bastards! What're you waiting for?" he screamed at them, and when no reply came, he grew angrier. "Come on, dammit, kill me then, get it over with!

But they didn't move, only the soft sounds of their dry skin rubbing against one another filled the night.

But then the ghouls made an opening and Tom looked up to the left to see Maria, with Brandon in her arms, staring down at him.

"You! You did this! Somehow, I don't know how, but you did this!"

Maria didn't reply to his accusations, she only stared at him, Brandon watching, too, both silent in their vigil.

And then she stepped away from the grave to let the undead have access. As if this was some silent signal, the ghouls began to fall into the grave, smothering Tom with their bodies.

At first he was smothered by them, but he fought back, screaming his rage as he struggled to overcome these undead creatures that shouldn't exist.

He punched and kicked, breaking bones and snapping off heads, but there were too many and eventually there were so many bodies in the grave with him there was no room to move; the sheer numbers pressing down on him, crushing him with their weight.

He felt fingernails sink into his abdomen, tearing his flesh open, pulling out the juicy organs waiting within and he screamed in utter agony.

He was in so much pain he could barely think. The ghouls began yanking out his liver, spleen and kidneys, then throwing them out of the grave so that all the other ghouls could have a piece of him.

As the ghouls were continuing to tear him apart piece by bloody piece, bit by bit, cracking his ribs like a starving man to a cooked chicken, Tom looked up through the shifting bodies smothering him and saw Maria and Brandon looking down, watching, their faces impassive.

But then, as he watched them, he saw their visages change and he could have sworn he saw his wife and son now smiling down on him with the same grin he used to give them after he gave them a beating.

He also thought he saw Maria mouth the words, "Rest in peace."

As Tom was looking up at them, two ghouls reached down and plucked out each of his eyeballs with their thumbs and their index fingers, shoving the respective white orbs into their mouths as white goo dripped out the sides of their cracked lips.

Tom's screams began to die down after long, agonizing minutes of torture, and as his heart was wrenched from his chest, his brain finally shutting down, he realized the last thing he would ever see in this world were the faces of his wife and son smiling at him in victory.

DOMENIC GIANGREGORIO

THE PORTAL

"Here we go again," Timmy Greenwich sighed as he felt himself falling.

Timmy only wanted a few more minutes of sleep, but his mom said that school started in five minutes. That was when Timmy rolled off the side of his bed and fell onto the kitchen floor which was the room under his bedroom.

"Timmy! How did you get down here?" his mother asked.

"It's a long and painful story," Timmy said while shaking his head.

His mother just shrugged, used to Timmy's antics.

She handed him a Pop-Tart and off to school he went.

When Timmy was at school, he slipped and went right through his desk chair, falling on his butt.

"Mr. Greenwich, stop it. Trying to be funny I see," his teacher said upon seeing his antics.

"I wasn't trying to be funny," explained Timmy. "Honest."

"Nonsense. Go right to the principal's office right now, Mr. Greenwich," ordered the teacher. "We've all had quite enough of your antics."

"But I didn't do anything," Timmy mumbled. The teacher just pointed towards the door.

While Timmy walked down the hallway, behind him a locker opened by itself, and an odd face with three eyes appeared. The face watched Timmy walk away. There were odd occurrences happening this day and Timmy had no idea he was in the middle of it.

Trudging down to the principal's office, Timmy soon found himself in detention.

It was while Timmy was in detention, the only one this day, that he saw a portal appear on the floor under the seat next to him.

"What's this?" Timmy wondered. It was as he stared at the black hole in the floor that the face appeared again.

A weird three-eyed monster popped out of it and grabbed Timmy's arm.

"Let go of me!" Timmy screamed.

Before Timmy could escape, the monster pulled him into the portal.

One second he was in school, and the next Timmy was flying right through asteroids and meteors in the vacuum of space. He was weightless.

"This is amazing," Timmy gasped.

"Hello there," said the three-eyed monster.

"Who're you?" Timmy asked.

"My name's Edgar," the monster replied. "Pleased to meetcha."

"What're we doing here?" Timmy asked. "Are you a monster?"

"No, not really. See, a couple of years ago when I was at the tender age of eleven, scientists did all sorts of tests on me to see if any of them would cause people to have strange powers," Edgar answered.

"What kind of powers do you have?" Timmy asked.

"Well, for one I'm able to teleport from place to place whenever I want," Edgar said. "And I can make things intangible."

"So me falling through the chair and falling through my bedroom floor was your doing?" Timmy said.

"Yup," Edgar replied.

"Why did you do that?" Timmy asked.

"Because you were the only one who can help me turn back to my human form," Edgar said.

"What turned you into this?" Timmy asked.

"When the scientists were working on me, a dose of a transforming liquid fell into the serum," Edgar explained.

"That's crazy," Timmy said, shocked. But then he looked around at the vastness of space and realized maybe it wasn't as crazy as it sounded.

Edgar ignored Timmy and continued.

"Then the serum was put into the tube and a shot was put into my arm. It spread through my body. The serum was the right one, though. Both of them mixed together and created my powers. Then I escaped."

Behind Timmy, floating in space was a hole, or more like a window. He could see his classroom through it and Edgar turned and aimed Timmy for the portal.

For the portal was about to close.

"You better get out of here before you get stuck in here forever," Edgar warned. Then he pushed Timmy at the portal.

Timmy flew towards the opening and he made it out in the nick of time.

As he fell into the classroom, the portal snapped shut as if it had never been there.

The teacher who had been out of the room, now returned and upon seeing Timmy on the floor, shook his head.

"Timmy Greenwich, just what am I going do with you?"

Timmy only smiled bashfully and climbed back into his chair to finish his hour of detention.

The next day.

It was lunch time and Timmy reached out to grab a tray from the stack by the lunch line.

But instead of grasping the tray, his hand slipped right through it. Luckily no one saw this. He decided he didn't need a tray and moved down the line.

When he went to get some pizza he picked up the dish but then the plate slipped through his fingers and he dumped it on himself. He didn't even know the dish was in his hand till it was gone.

"Trying to be funny again I see," Timmy's teacher said from behind him. All he'd seen is the pizza being dropped. "Looks like someone's going back to detention."

So Timmy got sent to detention again, but this time nothing happened.

No portal appeared. Simply nothing.

Then school was over and Timmy was sitting on the monkey bars in the playground, feeling disappointed that Edgar hadn't shown up.

"Hey, Timmy," Edgar whispered from behind him.

"Ah!" Timmy screamed, surprised. He was so startled he fell off the monkey bars.

"Are you okay?" Edgar asked.

"Yeah, I'm fine. Just a couple of bruises. Nothing to worry about," Timmy answered as he sat on ground. "Just don't sneak up on a guy, okay?"

"No problem," Edgar said and as he helped Timmy up. Then, before Timmy knew what was happening, Edgar tossed him into the portal.

"Thanks for nothing," Timmy said as he went into the portal.

"Don't mention it," Edgar said with a grin and jumped in behind him.

They floated through space and then Edgar opened another portal, this one leading to someplace new.

Edgar was bringing Timmy to the lab where he was mutated. So with Edgar leading the way, they both entered the portal.

But Edgar didn't have them go right into the main part of the lab. Instead, they ended up in a heating vent.

"It's hot in here," Timmy said wiping his face with his shirt.

"That's why they call it a heating vent, silly. Because it's hot," Edgar said.

They squeezed down the vent until they found the opening. There was a metal grate blocking the vent which overlooked the lab. Edgar looked down and saw a scientist. It was the same scientist that had done the tests on him that changed him.

"That's him," Edgar said.

"Who?" Timmy asked.

"The one who ran those tests on me. He's the one," Edgar answered.

As the scientist walked away to the opposite end of the lab, Edgar opened the metal grating and they popped out of the heating vent. Dropping to the floor, they ducked down and hid behind a desk.

"Good, everything's ready. Now it's time to test out my new serum," the scientist said as he stepped closer to a cage where a sad looking dog was huddled within.

As the scientist moved through the lab, his hip struck the desk Timmy and Edgar were hiding behind and a glass test tube fell off the desk. Edgar used his power to teleport the test tube away before it struck the floor and broke, which would alert the scientist they were there.

"Where did it go?" Timmy whispered.

"I don't know," Edgar replied.

Suddenly the test tube popped out of nowhere and landed on top of the scientist's head.

"Ow! Who did that?" the scientist asked, looking around the lab.

Timmy's nose began to itch and before he could stop himself, he sneezed, the scientist turning to see the two of them hiding.

"Run!" Edgar cried out.

Edgar and Timmy tried to elude the scientist by escaping back into the heating vent.

Before he could catch them, the two were back in the vent. Frustrated they had escaped; he went to the thermostat and turned up the heat.

"If you can't take the heat then get out of the kitchen," the scientist growled with an evil grin.

But Timmy couldn't take the heat and as he tried to scurry down the vent, the hot air became too much and he felt his hands burning. But he was crawling up hill and he felt himself slipping back down. Before he could stop himself, he was slipping out of the heating vent.

"Timmy!" Edgar screamed.

Timmy fell right into the scientist's waiting hands. With an evil laugh, the scientist brought Timmy over to one of his medical tables.

"Finally, another test subject," the crazed scientist laughed.

Helpless to stop the man, Timmy was soon strapped to a table.

"Let me go!" Timmy yelled.

The scientist held up a syringe and without waiting another second, he plunged it into Timmy's arm, the boy crying out in pain.

He had been infected with the serum. The serum mixed with his blood, turning Timmy into a four-armed freak. But one of the side effects was that the serum also gave Timmy the ability to hover over objects.

After shooting the needle into Timmy's arm, the scientist then turned away from him to go after Edgar who had popped out of the vent to try and help Timmy.

Now Edgar was in jeopardy.

Unfortunately, Timmy had turned into an evil monster. Unlike Edgar who was good and kind.

"I going to rip you apart, you weakling!" Timmy screamed at the scientist as he broke free of the straps holding him, his four hands flexing in anger.

Timmy jumped up and hovered over the scientist but when he saw Edgar, he turned and went for him instead.

Before Timmy could grab him, Edgar teleported to a light on the ceiling.

"I don't want to hurt you, Timmy," Edgar said.

"Really, that's weird. Because I want to hurt you," Timmy snarled.

"This is a superb way to get rid of the three-eyed monster and the new freak I created all at the same time," the scientist said while rubbing his hands with glee.

Timmy picked up a chair and tossed it at the ceiling, the chair hitting the light Edgar was on.

Edgar fell to the floor while dodging Timmy's fists.

"Stop it, Timmy. I'm your friend!" Edgar said nicely, trying to calm Timmy down.

Edgar teleported away into the air and then popped up behind Timmy. He tried to grab Timmy from behind but Timmy hovered away and then spun around and punched Edgar's face right into the ceiling. Pieces of tiles and plaster rained down to the floor.

"This is fun to watch," the scientist said clapping merrily as his two creations fought. There was a gleam in his eye that said he wasn't all there. He was a few beakers short of a full test tube kit.

Timmy grabbed a leg and hurled him on to the medical table then he drifted over to Edgar. He raised his hand to bring them down on Edgar's chest, but Edgar teleported away and Timmy landed on the empty table.

"Get away from that!" the scientist yelled.

But as Timmy hit the table, Edgar reappeared and strapped Timmy to it.

"This is for your own good, Timmy," Edgar said. "Trust me."

Edgar shoved another needle into Timmy's upper right arm and as the serum took affect, Timmy slowly began to turn back to normal.

"This is terrible!" the scientist screamed. "No, this is all wrong!"

Timmy changed and soon was back to his old self. He blinked up at Edgar and said, "I'm starving."

Edgar nodded, understanding the change had made Timmy's body crave nutrients.

"Do you want some veal?" Edgar asked.

"What's veal?" Timmy asked.

"Little baby tortured cows," Edgar answered.

"Eww, no, that's gross," Timmy said with disgust.

"No, he needs to change back!" the scientist screamed as he ran at Timmy with a syringe to change him back into the four-armed freak. As the scientist grew near, Edgar grasped the scientist and punched him, dazing him from the blow. Then Edgar strapped him to another table and stuck him with the same syringe he was going to use on Timmy.

Then he left him there.

"What are you doing? You can't do this to me!" the scientist screamed.

"Come on, Timmy. Let's go home," Edgar said. "You've been through enough."

"But what about you?" Timmy asked. "Don't we have to try and get you changed back to normal?"

"No, Timmy, I think I'm fine just the way I am. And you have to admit the teleporting powers are pretty cool," Edgar grinned, though because he was a three-eyed monster it looked more like a snarl.

"Yeah, I can understand that. I guess you're right. You know, I think I'm gonna miss the four arms and the hovering powers, too," Timmy said. "Those were pretty cool. Too bad I got mean when I changed, though."

Timmy tried to swing his arms to see if he could somehow get his four arms back. He also tried jumping in the air or jumping off of a desk to see if his hovering powers would come back.

"Nothing," Timmy said sadly.

"Don't push your luck, Timmy. It might just come back and bite you in the butt," Edgar laughed.

With the scientist spasming on the table as he changed into God knows what, Edgar opened a portal and they both jumped in, leaving the lab behind. As they floated through space, Timmy smiled. "You know, I think I'm starting to get used to this portal thing."

Edgar smiled back and they floated on until Edgar opened a portal to bring Timmy back home.

Back in the outside world, at the lab, the scientist was kicking to get out of his straps as he kept spasming and changing. By accident his right foot whacked another brand new serum that he'd never tried before. The serum opened and fell down and it landed on the scientist left ankle, just above the top of his shoe. The serum soaked into the sock and then went inside his shoe. It spread from his foot to the remaining parts of his body and then his skin began absorbing it. Now two serums were in his body and he screamed as they went to work, changing him.

Then something happened; something very bad happened. The serum was the *fire* experiment. It was one that would give someone fire powers.

The scientist's skin began to turn bright red and his eyes turned from brown to yellow with orange stripes across the pupils. As he began to glow like a burning log in a fireplace, the straps holding him down were burnt to ash.

Now free, the scientist stood up and laughed.

"Ha! This is the last time that I will ever be a scientist," the burning man said. "Now I'm so much more!"

The floor under him burned to bits and pieces as he walked around the lab, anything close to him melting.

"My new name will be...uhm. It's in my head. Uh. I know this. You know what? I'll think of one later. No wait, better yet, I have it. From now on people can just call me FIRE BURNER!" he yelled with maniacal glee.

Fire Burner walked slowly to the still open portal while on the other side of the portal, Edgar and Timmy hopped out. They landed in the front of Timmy's house. It was dead dark. The pinwheel on the front lawn was stationary; there was no wind to propel it. In the large picture window on the front of the house, Timmy's black cat named Magic hid behind the curtain.

"What's wrong with Magic?" Timmy asked. "He looks scared."

Edgar looked behind himself to see if it was clear and then got propelled into Timmy's front right window, teleporting at the last second so he didn't crash into the glass. It was the exact place where Magic was hiding and the cat jumped up and hissed at the sight of a three-eyed monster named Edgar.

No one was home at the moment as Timmy called out for his mom, so he ran into his house through the front door, then dashed up the stairs to his room. He wanted to show Edgar his favorite toy so he picked up his remote-control UFO spaceship that actually hovers in the air and began to play with the remote control. The toy flew down the stairs and ended up hitting the back of Edgar's head by accident.

"Ouch! What's this?" Edgar asked as he picked up the toy.

"Oops. Sorry, buddy," Timmy answered as he ran down the stairs and into the living room. "It hovers like I could do and I wanted to show you."

"Okay, well then let's take it outside where there's more room to play," Edgar suggested and then he made himself, Timmy and the toy disappear, teleporting them all back out to the front lawn.

But no sooner did they pop back onto the lawn then Edgar found himself getting attacked from behind. It was Fire Burner who had appeared at the same time through the portal which had just snapped shut behind him.

Fire burner stomped on Edgar's left hand with a laugh of victory.

"Hurts, doesn't it," Fire Burner taunted as he pushed Edgar's hand into the grass with his shoe.

"Not as much as this is going to hurt you," Edgar said as he got his right hand around and twisted Fire Burner's left foot into the air.

"Whoa!" Fire Burner yelled as he fell to the grass, his sizzling body burning the lawn. The only reason it didn't explode into flame was the grass was nice and green and wouldn't burn.

"Ohhh, I'm dizzy," Fire Burner said as he held a hand to his head.

Edgar got up and raised his hands, curling them into fists. It must have been some sight for the neighbors to see a three-eyed monster and a burning man fighting on Timmy's front lawn.

"Come on, Edgar, fight to the end!" Timmy cheered from the side.

"Easy for you to say. You're not fighting," Edgar added as he prepared to fight Fire Burner.

But when Edgar replied to Timmy he was distracted and as he wasn't paying attention, Fire Burner kicked Edgar in his back, sending him sprawling to the ground.

"This is the end, Edgar," Fire Burner laughed. "I finally have you. Now you'll pay for escaping my lab."

Fire Burner put as much heat as he could into his right fist, preparing to burn Edgar's heart out.

"No!" Edgar screamed.

Fire Burner raised his fist high and just as he was about to bring it down he was stopped. Edgar opened his eyes to see Fire Burner being sprayed with water, all of the water immediately evaporating as soon as it touched the burning man's body.

Edgar looked to see where the water was coming from and there was Timmy, the house's garden hose in his hand, the nozzle on high.

"No, what are you doing? Stop it!" Fire Burner screamed, his flames going out as he was doused with the cold water.

"Ha, got you now!" Timmy yelled as he moved closer, the water dousing Fire Burner's flames.

But then Timmy got too close and Fire Burner reached out and slapped Timmy out of the way. Timmy was knocked into the picture window, taking the hit head on. He bounced off the thick glass and fell to the grass, woozy.

"Timmy!" Edgar cried out in surprise and worry for his friend.

But Timmy was unconscious as he lay in the grass.

"You fool. You shouldn't have risked your own life for this one," Fire Burner laughed at Timmy.

"Stop it. Stop it right now!" Edgar yelled and then something happened to Edgar, something even Edgar didn't understand. Such was his worry for Timmy that his body began to change again.

Some weird bump was sprouting out of the middle of Edgar's chest.

"What's this?" Fire Burner wondered as he stared down at the bump on Edgar's chest.

Edgar looked up and then ripped his shirt open and both he and Fire Burner gasped in shock.

There was now a giant extra eye on Edgar's chest six inches wide and five inches tall.

The eye lid opened and then shined a bright light into the sky, as if it could make the sun rise. But then something else happened. It had been an overcast day and now the clouds moved away and the moist air disappeared.

Fire Burner and Edgar could see themselves clearly now as they faced one another.

"This is much better," Fire Burner said as he closed his fist. Now that he wasn't being sprayed with water, his hand began to glow as he rallied his heat power from within.

Edgar nodded his head up and down, seeing the hand glow with white hot fire.

"I agree," Edgar said as he climbed to his feet, his large eye blinking at Fire Burner. "But not today. We'll finish this another time."

With a scream of rage, Fire Burner attacked, shooting a ball of flame at Edgar.

Edgar dodged and Fire Burner's fire ball burned down a tree to the left of the house, the flames crackling and spitting as they consumed the tree in brilliant reds and oranges.

In Timmy's neighbor's backyard, a woman screamed, seeing the impossible and unbelievable battle taking place in front of her eyes.

"Missed me," Edgar said with a grin.

"This time I won't miss. My calculations are correct," Fire Burner said as he spun and aimed his glowing hand at Timmy who was even now trying to sit up, still dazed by the blow he'd received. In another second, Timmy would be nothing but burnt human flesh.

As Fire Burner threw his fire ball, Edgar teleported to Timmy's side, then took Timmy with him into thin air as the fire ball missed, driving into the green lawn to sizzle and die.

A portal opened near the sidewalk and Edgar and Timmy reappeared. As they both turned and looked at Fire Burner, they jumped into the portal, which then winked out just as Fire Burner tried to reach it.

"No! You won't escape me that easily!"

But the two were gone. How could he hope to find them?

Fire Burner reached into his pocket of his fireproof clothing and pulled out a small receiver. It was in a fireproof bag also so it could withstand the heat of Fire Burner's body, and as the burning man held it up so he could see it better, he saw it was beeping with an arrow pointing to the west.

Unknown to Timmy, the man had planted a tracker on him back at the lab when he had first given him the serum. It was inside his body and Timmy didn't even know it was there.

As the receiver beeped steadily, pointing in the direction the two had escaped to, the former scientist turned evil villain nodded and laughed.

"I know where they are," Fire Burner explained. "And I'll find them."

ANTHONY GIANGREGORIO

ALONE

The battery-powered alarm clock began shrieking, seeming like a bomb about to explode if it wasn't given the attention it was asking for.

Brian Williams slammed his hand down on the top buttons, silencing the infernal shriek forever or until the next morning.

Immediately silence descended like a thunderclap and he let out a low moan, similar to what a zombie would make from the horror movies he used to watch when he was a kid.

He laid perfectly still, staring up at the ceiling of his home, wondering if today would be any different than the dozens before it.

At first, fogged from sleep, nothing really settled in, but then it all came back and he felt the loneliness overwhelm him.

He was so alone, dammit.

No one called him and no one sent him mail.

Sometimes he wondered if it was his fault, maybe he should just try and get out there more, you know, to meet new people, but then he would brush the idea away as foolish.

After all, he was a nice guy, why did he have to go out and seek their friendship? Why couldn't they come to him?

He lay in bed for more than ten minutes and then rolled out of bed with another groan and stood up, stretching heartily as his muscles and bones snapped and cracked.

Walking to the end of the bed, he began his regiment of exercises, knowing it would be the only thing to wake him up. He began with thirty pushups then went into crunches, then did a few curls to work on his abdomen. After that he did fifty jumping jacks, smiling the entire time. They always reminded him of high school gym as he jumped up and down, causing a few odds and ends on the nearby shelves to shake slightly.

Finished with his calisthenics, he padded to the small bathroom and took a shower. The water pressure sputtered once or twice and he cursed the damn plumbing in his house, but then it began to flow and soon the bathroom was filled with a wet, warm mist.

Climbing in the shower, he lathered up with soap, then used the small, circular mirror in front of him to shave. As he did so, he stared at the dark green eyes glaring back at him and he wondered if he would ever get to gaze into another's eyes again. But love had never been his forte and he could only hope the future would bring someone into his life.

Stepping out of the shower, now clean and shaved, he toweled off and then headed back to his bedroom. Not one for doing laundry, he dug through a pile of clothing until he found a shirt and pants that weren't too far over the edge of good taste.

Besides, it's not like anyone would be smelling him today, but then he could always hope.

Whenever he left the house, he always hoped he would meet someone nice, strike up a friendship and then he wouldn't be so alone, but so far no one had popped up.

With a small sigh after dressing, he headed to his kitchen and made himself some coffee and toast, the bread coming from the freezer.

As the coffee was percolating, he went to the answering machine and frowned when all it said was zero.

No one had called as he slept and why would they? It was like he was a pariah, no one wanted his company.

When the toast and coffee were ready he ate silently at the table, glancing through an old newspaper more than two months old. He didn't mind, it was something to pass the time and he could have cared less that the news was out dated.

Finally finished with breakfast, he walked into his den and stared at the pictures on the walls. His parents' faces smiled back at him and he missed them terribly, knowing both had died a few months ago. Another picture grinned back next to his parents' photo. It was of his brother, but he didn't know where is brother was. The man had never called, so as far as Brian was concerned the man was as good as dead to him.

There was a small trophy on the shelf to his right and he walked to it, picking it up with an awful sigh of longing. He had won this at the company picnic a year ago. He remembered getting close to Tricia that day. She was one of the many drones in accounting, but she was pretty and smart and acted like she liked him. But now, more than three months after he'd left his job, she had never called once. He knew he shouldn't feel rejected by her as they had never made any kind of commitment, but he'd just felt like they had made that connection, the one that says two people might have a chance together.

Oh, well, all water under the bridge now, he figured.

There were many other fish in the sea, his father used to say, the question was, did he have the right bait to catch one?

Leaving the den, he walked back into the kitchen. There was a pile of bills sitting on the counter, one for the mortgage from more than four months ago. He wasn't worried about paying it, he knew the banks had enough trouble right now and they could come take his home if they had a problem with him. Besides, all it would take would be one phone call and he would gladly pay the bill, hell, he would do cartwheels if they called him.

But know one called him anymore and he knew they might never.

He didn't know what was wrong with him, but everyone had turned their backs on him. He sometimes wondered who he had offended but nothing came to mind.

God, maybe, maybe he'd offended God and this was his punishment.

Deciding he shouldn't think like that, as it wasn't productive, he went to the front hallway and prepared to go out for another day on the town. As he got ready, he wondered if today would be the day he would meet someone new.

He kicked the junk mail to the side where it had sat for months, not interested in it. There were a few he recognized such as the weight loss one and the one where if he took just one small pill a day he would end up with a massive penis to please the ladies.

He ignored them all and he didn't feel like picking them up.

Let the maid do it, he thought with a chuckle.

Going to the hall closet, he opened it slowly, reached inside, and took out his coat. It was heavy leather jacket with pieces of thin metal sewn into the lining to reinforce it. It was long, to his ankles, and dark black with many pockets. Sliding his arms through the sleeves, he relished the feeling of the heavy material on his shoulders; the smell of the worn leather.

Then he reached into the closet and began taking out the things most people would probably use before going out into his new world.

The first item was a pump action shotgun, the butt worn from use, the barrel splattered with dried blood. The second item was a police issue Glock, taken from a cop who didn't need it anymore. The seventeen round clip was full, thanks to the boxes of ammunition stacked in the top shelf of the closet, and he ejected the clip and checked it, then popped it back in. It never hurt to double check.

One bullet could mean the difference between life and death.

The next item was a long, eighteen inch machete with a wooden grip that had been wrapped with electrical tape to help when his palm got sweaty. The blade was razor sharp and looked like it had already gotten a fait bit of use.

This he hung from his belt, the rope looped through a hole in the handle. It had no sheath and hung free.

The last thing he pulled from the closet was a riot helmet, the top scuffed and scratched from use. Strapping it on, he began running his hands over his body, making sure everything was in place and easy to reach. The Glock was on his right hip, the shotgun he would carry, and the machete was on his left side, swinging gently as he moved about the hallway.

He took a few boxes of shotgun shells out of the closet and dropped them into his voluminous pockets, then checked the shotgun itself to make sure it was loaded.

Ejecting the first shell, he then popped it back in, feeling confident he was ready for anything.

He turned and glanced back through the hallway to the kitchen table, and spotted his breakfast plate and coffee mug still there. He'd forgotten to place them in the sink.

Oh, well, they'd be there when he retuned this evening, he knew that for a fact.

Reaching into his left pocket, he pulled out a pair of heavy leather gloves, then slid them on with practiced ease. The knuckles of the gloves were reinforced with small ball bearings and did havoc to a human face if used properly.

So armed and ready, the heavy leather of his jacket like a light-weight Kevlar covering his body, he opened his front door and gazed out into the sun-drenched street of his neighborhood.

Though his grass was high and his bushes were wild, he wasn't worried about his neighbors complaining.

Stepping out onto the cement landing, he closed the front door behind him and prepared to start his day.

With a casual gait, he walked down his pathway and in seconds was in the street.

Maybe today I'll find someone, he hoped as he turned and let out a low whistle.

Immediately, ten shambling forms at the end of the street turned at his call and began to stumble towards him.

Pumping the shotgun, he stood in the middle of the street, his leather jacket billowing in the gentle breeze.

He planned on working his way to the south side of town today, and then double back before night fall.

God, I'm so alone, he thought for the hundredth time. *Surely there has to be someone else alive out here in this giant, undead world.*

As the zombies stumbled closer, the gaping wounds and pale, desiccated frames reaching for him, he got to work.

It had been a lonely existence for the past few months since the dead began to walk and swallowed the world whole, but he wasn't about to give up.

Like he'd been doing for months, each day he would head out in search of survivors. And when he found them he knew life would be just a little bit better.

He shot the first two zombies in their faces, sending skull and brain matter across the pavement to twinkle in the sun, and he quickly followed that with three more shots, taking out the rest. Then he swung the shotgun over his shoulder and pulled the machete, wanting to conserve ammo when possible. He'd gotten most of them quickly and now the numbers weren't so bad. They were slow and he was fast and he could take them down easily.

Then he would head out for the hundredth time to search for survivors like himself.

As he took down the last zombie in line, slicing its head in half and kicking the corpse to the road, he set off without a backwards glance to the fetid cadavers now sprawled on the road like road kill.

The crows came out of the sky almost immediately to begin feeding on the rotting meat, but Brian never noticed. All he knew was what was in his mind, his heart, and what had picked at him for what seemed like forever.

And that was how truly alone he was.

DOMENIC GIANGREGORIO

STAYING HOME

"Good Evening! This is reporter William Strong here. It seems that a meteorite is going to hit the middle of Rosemont Terrace in ten hours," the reporter said. *"Right where the Johnson house is located."*

At the Johnson house, in the middle of Rosemont Terrace, Jimmy watched the news, his eyes going wide at the reporter's words.

"Ahh! Oh my God!" Jimmy screamed.

Jimmy's mom and dad ran into the living room in a hurry to see Jimmy pointing at the television in shock.

"What happened?" Jimmy's dad asked.

"There's a meteorite coming to Earth and it's going to hit our house in ten hours!" Jimmy explained excitedly. "We have to get out of here!"

"Now, now, son, a lot of people have the same last name as us," Jimmy's dad said calmly.

"To confirm the previous report. The meteorite is going to hit the Johnson's house in nine hours and fifty-six minutes," reporter William Strong said.

I'm sure it's not our house, Jimmy," Jimmy's dad said.

"The meteorite will hit Jimmy Johnson's house on 54 Danger Street," reporter William Strong said.

"That's where we live!" Jimmy's mom screamed.

"It can't be. I'm sure it's just another house with the name Johnson that's also on 54 Danger Street. They must live right down the street. Wow, they've been right on top of us all this time and we never knew it," Jimmy's dad said.

"Dad. It's our house they're talking about in TV. It has to be," Jimmy said.

It took some more convincing but eventually his dad gave in.

Jimmy's family packed everything up and left their home.

But for some inexplicable reason, right when they left their street they were immediately teleported back to their house.

"What happened?" Jimmy's dad wondered.

"It seems that we've been teleported back to our house right after we left our street," Jimmy said.

"I guess that's why they call this street Danger Street," Jimmy's mom said.

"The meteorite will hit the Johnson's house on 54 Danger Street in nine hours and twenty three minutes," reporter William Strong said.

"Losing oxygen. Can't breathe," Jimmy's mom gasped as she stood in the living room, her hands clutching to her throat.

"What are you doing?" Jimmy asked.

"Nothing, honey, I just wanted to make a scene," Jimmy's mom replied with a grin.

"We need an idea," Jimmy said. "We need to do something."

"Well at least we have nine hours and twenty two minutes to figure something out," Jimmy's dad said.

"Oh, wait, I almost forgot. It seems that it's spring and we have to turn our clocks forward nine hours and twenty-two minutes and fifty five seconds," reporter William Strong said.

"I hate my life," Jimmy said.

The meteorite struck his house and killed them all.

ANTHONY GIANGREGORIO

MOMMA'S BOY

"Harold! Get up here, I need changing again! Harold!"

The shrill voice filled the house, seeming to slice the air like a dagger through flesh. The voice floated from the second floor bedroom, down the hallway, and then down the old worn wooden stairs. The voice floated through the dark house, all the shades drawn, and finally settled on the young man sitting at the dining room table, with hands clenched into fists.

His knuckles were white with the pressure as the face of the young man cringed at the sound of his name.

"Harold! Did you hear me?"

And then, to add insult to injury, a bell began to chime. A tingling bell that should remind him of Christmas, but instead it drove him crazy. To him, the bell was the sound of death.

He would like to think it would be his mother's death, but the truth was he didn't think the old crone would ever die.

Stricken with a debilitating illness, she had been wasting away for almost seven long years now and every time he thought she finally expired, she would open her eyes and snap at him.

Oh, yes, she would snap at him. Instead of being grateful that her only son had given up his life to take care of her, she constantly belittled him, nagging and poking at him like a crow would at the open wound of a corpse.

She never let up, he never did anything right. If he made her soup it was too hot or too cold. If he made her a sandwich the cut in the bread was off. If he made her pudding there was too much milk in it. He could never please her and though at one time he did love her, as a dutiful son should; now all he wanted was her dead.

But he was too much of a coward to do it.

"Harold!" This followed by that damn bell, the tinkling filling his brain like an ice pick.

With a deep sigh of regret, he relaxed his fists, the skin tone returning to normal, and he stood up from his chair.

"Coming, Mother!" He called as he began walking to the kitchen.

The clock on the wall said it was 6:10 pm and he knew she wanted her evening tea. She was very predictable, his mother. She would eat lunch at precisely 12:30, then at 2 pm she would have a bowel movement, one Harold would then have to clean. She wouldn't use a bedpan, and Harold had to change her like she was a one-year-old, the large diapers wrapped around her skin and bones like bandages on a mummy.

He thought she did it to belittle him even more than she already did. She could use a bedpan if she preferred, but she liked the idea of her son having to wipe her ass.

Then, at 5:30 pm she would have her supper, which usually consisted of something light.

And then, finally, at 6:10 she would have tea with a cookie or something sweet.

As Harold prepared her tea, he had dark thoughts of slipping in something poisonous. He imagined her sipping the tea, telling him how too hot or cold it was, then she would suddenly stop talking, drop the tea to her lap as she began to spasm. She would roll her eyes and reach for her throat as she gasped her one final breath of air. But then a dry rasp would come from her open mouth and she would slump forward, dead at last.

But he knew that wouldn't be happening. He watched enough crime shows to know if he poisoned her they would know it.

No, he just had to wait for nature to take its course, no matter how many more years that would be.

"Harold, damn you, boy, where the hell is my tea?"

Pulled from his reverie, he finished making the tea, added a couple of Graham crackers to the tray and slowly plodded up the stairs.

As he walked through the gloom-filled house, his eyes scanned the pictures on the wall hanging haphazardly, most crooked. They were crooked because he didn't have the energy to fix them. He never left the house, as he was now a full time nurse. His mother had a wealthy bank account, the stipend more than enough to support them both for many years to come.

"Harold, where are you, boy?"

"Coming, Mother, I'm almost there," he called as he began walking up the stairs, the boards creaking with each footstep. There were more pictures here as well, some with his father in them. But the man had left when Harold was just a boy, barely five, the man not able to deal with his shrew of a wife any longer.

And so Harold had become husband, son and best friend to his mother, and sometimes, when she had been younger and more amorous, she'd come into his bedroom late at night when he was asleep and crawled into his bed. Then, hands would go places they should never go and he had become so much more than just a son for her. And it made him feel dirty every single day of his life until she finally stopped.

He had no friends, as he was home schooled, and truth be told, to him, there wasn't a life outside the dark walls of his house. Though he wished for his mother's death, at the same time it frightened him.

What would he do when she was finally gone?

"Hurry up, Harold, it's almost 6:15," she said from the bedroom.

"Yes, Mother," he replied as he reached the top of the stairs and entered her bedroom.

The odor of death permeated the room, or the odor of death waiting in the wings for its time to arrive. Harold barley noticed this; the redolence of decay had been hanging in the air of the bedroom for so long it was as natural to him as detecting salt on an ocean breeze.

Standing in the doorway, he gazed across the room at his mother.

"Well, it's about time, Harold. What were you doing down there, Mmm? Looking at those dirty magazines I bet, filthy boy,"

"Yes, Mother."

As he crossed the room with the tray, he took in his mother's gaunt appearance. She was so frail she looked like she was dead already, but the fire in her eyes belayed that. Her skin was tight against the skull, the bone protruding in places so that it looked like you might cut yourself if you rubbed her face too hard with your palm. Her hands were like brittle claws, curved and gnarled like old tree branches. Dark warts and liver spots covered her flesh to the point the original, flesh tone was gone forever. As he moved closer, he detected the ammonia of urine.

Great, she's pissed herself again, he thought.

"Give it here, boy, it's almost too late now," she barked as he set the tray on her lap. She was sitting up, one of the few things she could still do without help, but leaving the bed was practically impossible. For bathing, when she would allow one, he would carry her and use the special chair setup in the shower stall.

But no sooner would she be clean and bathed then an hour later she would smell like urine or shit herself again, all that work for nothing.

Her buttocks and back were covered with bed sores, most weeping a yellow pus that never seemed to stop. The sheets were crusted like moldy bread and a pungent odor hovered around her like bees to a flower.

"Here you are mother, just the way you like it," he said as he left the tray and stepped back.

She gazed at the tea, then without preamble picked it up and as she raised it to her lips she looked at Harold.

"I hope it has the right amount of sugar in it."

"Yes, Mother," he replied, knowing there was nothing else to say that would please her.

She sipped the tea, and no sooner had the liquid touched her lips then she spit it out, followed by tossing the steaming liquid at her son, though she still held onto the tea cup.

"Damn it, boy, it's too cold! Get me another one!"

Harold screamed as the scalding tea landed on his lower torso and crotch. At first the tea seared his flesh, but soon it was cooling, but he knew when he undressed that night he would have red welts where the tea had touched his flesh after seeping through his clothes.

"And change your clothes, your all wet," she demanded. "But not until you get me another cup, and this time make sure it's hot!"

Panting from the pain, he stepped to her and took the tray, wincing as he moved his legs.

"Yes...Mother," he gasped.

She shook her head, her stringy, greasy hair shifting slightly.

"Such a weak thing you are, Harold, no wonder your father left you. He was ashamed of having such a pathetic son."

Gritting his teeth, he nodded. "Yes, Mother, I suppose so. I'll be right back with a fresh cup," he said as he walked way.

"And get me some of those biscuits I like, not those damn graham cracker cookies. You like those, not me!" She called after him. "Damn fool of a boy."

He hunched his shoulders as he listened and then continued onward, back down the stairs, passing the family photos and back into the kitchen.

As he began making more tea, wincing each time he moved, he could hear some noise coming from the street in front of the house. It sounded like screams, then a crash of metal on metal, followed by a car horn. The horn was blaring, but then it stopped and he was about to go check, wondering what might be happening, when his mother's voice filled the house.

"Harold! Harold! Make sure you get the sugar right this time, too!"

Thinking of checking what was going outside was forgotten as his mother's voice penetrated his mind. Focusing on the tea, he got to work again and in no time was slowly climbing the stairs once again.

As he did, he thought of his childhood years, and how his mother had treated him. She had never really treated him as her son, no, he was more like her pet, there for whatever she needed him to be. Whether it was a lover, a maid, or a confidant, he was always there for her. Deep down he did love her, he had to, she was his mother after all, but there was something else there, too, something that had been growing for so many years it was a part of him.

Hate, pure unadulterated hate for another living person.

As he reached her room, she was waiting for him. She had the TV on, and she impatiently flicked through the channels. The news was on every channel, people talking about a crisis, about people attacking others. But no sooner did Harold hear a few words, tidbits, then she shut off the television and tossed the remote away from her.

"Ah, all fools, damn country. When I was young, my generation knew how to do things," she looked to Harold. "Not like you and others your age. They're all fools, Harold, running this country to the ground. You should listen to me; I know what I'm talking about."

"Yes, Mother," he said softly, not wanting to get her started. To her, everything in the world was his fault. His *generation* as she called it. He took it all with a stiff upper lip, but deep down it made him want to scream, or cry, or both.

"Ah, good, my tea, now let's see if you got it right this time."

He answered by setting the tray on her lap again, the tray wobbling for a moment.

He stepped back again, but not as far as last time, thinking the tea had to be fine. He had boiled it to the point there was nothing left of the water in the pot, and had then rushed up here as fast as he could once he'd poured it. Water was not able to be made hotter by standard means and he was confident she would be pleased.

So when she took a sip and with a snarl tossed the scalding tea into his face, he lost it, his mind finally cracking from all the abuse and torture he'd suffered under his mother's hands.

With a yell, blinded by the scalding liquid, he reached out and wrapped his hands around her frail neck.

"Harold, what are you doing?" She squawked. "Release me at once!"

But Harold wasn't listening anymore. Now lost in rage, all that was left was an abused man who'd had enough.

"No, Mother, not this time, now it's time to die!" Harold screamed loudly, his mouth curved up in rage as he squeezed the life out of her. She began to gasp, her tongue protruding, then she began to beat her hands at him.

A small part of his mind realized if he strangled her people would know, they could tell, so he let her neck go and then grabbed a pillow, then climbed on top of her, sitting on her lap like she had done to him time and again in the middle of the night.

He pressed down on the pillow, her face now lost under the feathered material and her legs kicked and fluttered behind him and her arms waved, her hands trying to find his face.

Her right hand managed to find his cheek and nails raked his flesh, leaving a deep, bloody gash. But Harold ignored the pain, his face already bright red from the hot tea. His eyes were blurry from either being burned or it was just a killing lust, but still he pressed, putting all of his weight on the single pillow.

At first she fought him, body jerking, but soon she began to tire as her lungs struggled for oxygen. Then, as he prayed it would happen, she finally stopped moving and her arms fell to her sides and she became immobile.

Breathing hard, panting like a dog, he still pressed, not believing she could actually die. She was like a demon from Hell, never fully destroyed, but always returning just when you thought you were free.

He stayed on top of her, pushing the pillow onto her face for almost five minutes, like a statue frozen in time, and then he blinked and sat back, taking the pillow off her face.

And there she was, dead at last.

He mouth was parted, her tongue slightly poking out, her eyes still open but seeing nothing. Her skin was taut and he could detect the odor of yet more offal and urine, the woman evacuating her bowels and bladder in death.

So, she was finally dead. He had done something he never thought he would have the guts for and yet here it was.

He was free, finally free.

"Mother?" He said, expecting her eyes to snap forward and then her words to attack him once more, but nothing happened, her face was stiff from death.

Checking her neck, he was relieved to see there was barely a mark there. No matter how hard he had squeezed, the wattled, off color skin more than hid any telltale marks of strangulation. Besides, he had stopped and switched to the pillow long before he could have done any serious damage...he hoped.

She looked almost like she was sleeping, but with her eyes open, so he reached out and closed them, still expecting her to turn her head and belittle him again. As he closed her eyes, his hand began to shake and he climbed off the bed, feeling the first stages of shock seeping in.

But despite this, he felt like he was the happiest man alive, like he had been given a life sentence in Hell and was suddenly released for no apparent reason.

A chuckle came to his mouth, filling the room and it sounded wrong somehow. Laughter wasn't allowed in this room, now or before. Feeling guilty, he left the room after glancing one last time at his mother.

He thought he should go cover her with a sheet, but decided against it. No, better it looked like she had died in her sleep and he hadn't touched her at all.

It wouldn't be hard to act like he was grieving for her, for there was a small part of him, the child of so many years ago, that was going to miss her.

Though she was a shrew, she was his mother, his only mother in this life, and now she was gone.

Sighing heavily, he went to the bathroom, cleaned up and then went to the phone to call the coroner, the entire time fighting to keep the hint of a smile that kept trying to appear on his face.

He was actually free!

"Oh, Harold, I'm so sorry for your loss," the night nurse said from the hospital at the other end of the phone call. "But we don't have anyone available to get your mother right now. The coroner's up to his eyeballs in bodies tonight."

"What do you mean you can't come get her? She's dead. That's what you do right? When someone dies you're supposed to get them," he said into the phone.

The nurse didn't say anything to him for a moment, as she dealt with something Harold couldn't see. The nurse knew Harold and his mother well from the times he'd brought his mother in for checkups when she wasn't feeling well. Of course later, she was at the point she was bedridden and never went back, but the town was small and the nurse knew Harold well as the dutiful son who looked after his ailing mother.

"I know that, Harold but there's something weird going on tonight. People are acting crazy. Haven't you been watching the news?"

"No," Harold replied. "Mother doesn't like me watching the news. She says it's all lies put there by the mass media."

"Oh, well, I see, look, Harold, I have to go, it's a madhouse here." Then her voice sounded far away as she spoke to someone. "Oh my God, he looks horrible, what happened, did someone bite him? Put him over there, Lisa?" Then she was back on the phone. "Harold, I have to go, I promise we'll get the coroner there as soon as we can, until then, well, once again I'm so sorry for your loss, your mother was a...sweet woman."

Harold almost laughed then remembering how awful his mother was to the hospital staff. Almost as bad as she treated him.

"All right, well, I'll be here waiting, thanks for your..." he stopped because the line was dead, the nurse had hung up.

Setting the phone back in its cradle, he went and made himself a cup of tea, thinking of his mother as he did so. No more tea, no more wiping her ass, no more listening to her belittle him.

It was hard to believe it was truly over.

Despite this weight lifted from his shoulders, another part of him was still saddened. Even though she could be cruel, she was his mother and now she was gone.

Going into the living room, he sat down and sipped his tea. He glanced up at the sound of someone yelling outside, but decided it was none of his business. No one would come to his house for help if there was something happening outside, he knew this with a certainty. And at the moment though, he could have cared less, lost in his inner turmoil of loss and happiness at the exact same time.

Guilt riddled his mind for what he did, but at the same time he felt good about it, like standing up to a bully in the schoolyard and winning, and then becoming the hero of the school.

The entire neighborhood knew to stay away from this particular house. The **No Trespassing** signs scattered around the property were there to make sure of it, too.

When his tea was done and his adrenalin had worn off, he felt himself becoming drowsy, and before he realized it he'd drifted off into a restless slumber.

As he dreamed, visions of his mother came to him. She was young again and she was good to him. This was before the disease had begun withering her body away and changing her personality into something as deformed as her bent figure. Of course, back then he didn't know there was any other way to live. He assumed everyone had a mother like his.

Hours later, he snapped awake and in the darkness of the room staggered to his feet, then flipped on a light.

He could hear the sounds of sirens and yells from somewhere outside, but it didn't sound close like before. A few fireworks, or what sounded like fireworks, could be heard in the distance, or maybe it was a car backfiring.

Or maybe it was gunshots? No, that would be ridiculous.

The lamp in the corner banished the darkness and he saw by the clock on the mantle it was well past midnight and close to morning. As the fugue of sleep left his mind, he realized no one had shown up to take his dead mother away.

Walking up the stairs, he entered her bedroom again. In the shadows, he could see her shape outlined, and it looked like she was sleeping once more. He could almost imagine he heard her breathing as she sucked in one more ounce of air.

Turning on the small lamp by her bedside, he gazed down at her still form. He reached out and touched her throat to make sure she was still dead and breathed a sigh of relief to see there was no pulse.

For some reason he just wanted to make sure she was dead, as if it had all been a dream and she was still alive and well.

But, no, she was dead, her blue complexion and swollen tongue the evidence of that.

Turning, he went back downstairs and called the hospital again, wanting to know where the damn coroner was, but this time all he received for his trouble was a busy signal. He hung up three times and redialed, but each time he got the same droning signal.

Disgusted, he hung up the phone and went to the sink for a glass of water, then searched for the bottle of aspirin he kept in a drawer. His head was pounding and he swallowed three at once, hoping it would stop the jackhammer rattling around in his brain.

Not knowing what to do, he dimmed the light and went back to the couch, figuring he would just have to wait until morning and then he could try the coroner again. Surely whatever was happening was isolated and by morning it would all be sorted out.

He considered going to change, but was too exhausted to bother and his clothes had dried partially thanks to his body heat.

Soon, with the aspirin taking affect, he drifted off to sleep again, nightmare visions of his dead mother's face haunting him.

He snapped awake again an hour later, but he didn't know what had awoken him. Looking around the room, it was the same as before, but he knew he'd heard something, as if a person had called his name.

And then he heard it again. And as when did, his testicles slid up into his abdomen and his blood went cold as he gasped in fear and disbelief.

"Harold, where are you? Where's my damn tea?"

The voice was like dead leaves rustling in the trees in late autumn, a hoarse, dry rasp, like crackling paper.

"Mother?" He gasped impossibly. "But it can't be, you're dead," he whispered.

He waited to hear her voice again and when it didn't come he tried to tell himself he must have imagined it. After all, he'd seen her corpse, she was as dead as dead could be. This was just his guilt making him suffer and imagine things.

"Harold! Where the hell are you, boy? Give me my tea! It's time for my tea!"

No, he'd heard it that time, it was real; it wasn't in his head.

Swallowing the knot in his throat, he stood on shaky legs. His bladder was holding on by a shoestring and he forced himself to stay calm. Something inside of him shriveled into a ball, then. It was the freedom he thought he'd won, now snuffed out like a candle in a thunderstorm.

And then the ringing began, the damn ringing of the bell that drove him slowly mad.

The voice now joined the ringing until they seemed to blend into one voice.

"*Harold!*"

Ring, ring, ring.

"*Harold!*"

"I...I'm coming, Mother!" He called as he slowly crept towards the stairs.

He began climbing them one at a time, the shadows across the pictures twisting the faces into macabre reflections of what they had been in daylight.

As he reached the top landing, the voice and ringing became louder.

"Harold, damn you, boy, bring me my tea!"

He stepped into her bedroom and let out a gasp of shock.

There she was, sitting up, waving her hand as the bell tinkled back and forth. But she wasn't exactly how she had been before.

Her head was lolling to the side and the handprints of where he had squeezed her neck and crushed her windpipe were now prevalent. It had taken lividity to show the marks post mortem. Her limbs were stiff from rigor, but she worked her way through it, her bones seeming to crack each time she rang the bell.

"Mother? But how...?"

"*How the hell should I know, boy, now where's my tea? You damn fool, you came up and didn't bring it? You tried to kill me, don't think you won't pay for that. I'll make your life a living hell from now on!*"

"I...I'm sorry, Mother, I lost control. I'm glad you're all right. I'll go get your tea right away," he said as he turned and ran down the stairs while she called him names and cursed his ever being born.

Downstairs in the kitchen, Harold moved about as he prepared her tea, his mind frozen in shock. He was on automatic, his brain unable to register what was happening. He'd seen her, she was dead; there had been no question in his mind about it.

She had been dead!

When the tea was prepared, he dropped a tea bag into the hot water and carried the tray up like he'd done so many times before.

He barely felt the dampness of his clothing as he climbed the shadow enshrouded stairs. He didn't need more light, having gone up and down the stairs so many times he knew where every piece of wood was and how it would react to his weight on it.

Upon entering the room, the redolence of death was stronger now, more like rotting meat, and he scrunched up his nose at the smell.

Walking over to her, he set the tray down and then stepped back. She wasn't paying attention to him, however, as she had turned on the TV and was watching a news report.

"...and at this time, we have reports, unbelievable as it seems, that the recently dead are returning to life and are able to function in a similar capacity as before they passed away. Reports are coming from all over the world, that this is not an isolated..." she turned off the television and threw the remote to the bed.

"Bah, fools, the dead are coming back to life. What do they take us for, idiots? Damn mass media." She sipped her tea and when it wasn't to her liking, she threw it at Harold who yelped in pain as he felt his skin bubble from where she'd scalded him earlier that night.

"Damn it, boy, can't you do anything right? It's too hot this time, now get me another cup! We can do this all night until you get it right!"

Still thinking about the news report, he nodded in a daze. "Yes, Mother, right away," he said as he picked up the tea cup near his feet and took the tray from her lap to make her a fresh cup.

He went down the stairs slowly, like a man who was being led to a lifetime prison sentence, and in a way he was.

For you see, Harold had always tried to keep that small bit of hope alive inside him, knowing that one day, eventually, his mother would die and then he would be free, but now...

Well, he had just discovered that he chose to kill his mother on the one night, of all nights, when the dead were returning to life.

He'd just resigned himself to a lifetime of taking care of her as she now could *never* die. And if he decided to kill himself to end it all, he would only come back and remain her slave for all eternity.

He was truly trapped even worse than before, though impossible as that was to believe.

And as he began to boil a new pot of water for her tea, and she began calling him again in her hoarse voice, the bell ringing like a bell tower of doom, he began to laugh, a hard, manic laugh that set his chest on fire and made him cough between bouts.

And as his laughter grew louder and louder, he prayed it would somehow drone out the sound of her voice and the infernal bell, because he planned on laughing until his voice grew raw and he finally made his mind snap, for this night, the only salvation for him would be insanity and the only freedom for him was to lose his mind forever.

But even as he slowly tried to lose his mind to madness, his mother's shrill, hoarse voice seeped into his brain, boring into his head like a massive drill, and he knew he would never be free of her and would be her prisoner to the end of time.

"Harold, where's my damn tea!"

Harold slumped to the floor and wept.

DOMENIC GIANGREGORIO

LIKE FATHER, LIKE SON

It was a beautiful sunny day, the sky a bright blue.

Deep below the surface of one particular lake, even the fish were as happy as clams.

Everyone was happy and enjoying the day, well, except for Eddy.

It was Saturday and Eddy was always grumpy on Saturdays.

"I hate Saturdays," Eddy mumbled.

Every Saturday, Eddy would take his electrical box filled with batteries and wires and he would throw it into the lake.

It would always make the fish very mad.

"Why does he always dump his electrical box into our lake?" Benny the fish gargled.

The electrical box is big every week. But this week it was huge. Everyone in Eddy's house was using electricity every hour of every day. Eddy wouldn't stop watching television. Betty (Eddy's wife) wouldn't stop using the vacuum to clean every part of the house. Peter (Eddy's son) wouldn't stop playing video games. And Kim (Eddy's daughter) wouldn't stop blow drying her hair.

Benny the fish got every fish in the lake to help stop the electrical box from touching the bottom of the lake. But even with all of them there still wasn't enough fish in the lake to hold up the electrical box.

"We're too weak!" Benny the fish yelled.

The electrical box fell down and touched the bottom. When it touched the muddy floor there was a huge explosion. The explosion was so big that it knocked Eddy up out of the water and into the air, then all the way to Mount Everest...or so it seemed.

Eddy was unconscious for thirty minutes. When he woke up he found a hundred fish lying in his canoe and staring up at him. Eddy was surprised that the canoe didn't sink, especially since there were easily a hundred fish in the canoe.

"Good fishys, nice fishys," Eddy said, frightened.

One of the fish stood up on its rear fin, moved forward a bit, and said one thing.

"This is the last time you're ever, and I mean ever, going to throw your heavy electrical boxes into our lake again. Do you hear me, fool?" Mr. T Fish shouted at Eddy.

Both species, man and fish, looked at each other continuously until something crazy and enormous happened. A meteorite struck Mount Everest off in the distance. The meteorite was red and black all over and was hot to the touch. The shaking of the earth and water made Eddy and all the fish fall out of the canoe.

It was a long and hurtful fall into the water but luckily they fell into the lake. The fish were underwater and now so was Eddy!

The fish said three words. And those three words were "WE'LL GET YOU!"

Eddy heard them somehow and at the same time realized he couldn't breathe. He tried to swim for the surface, but the fish stopped him.

"Oh, no, my boy. You aren't going anywhere," Benny the fish said.

Eddy never learned how to swim so that was a bad problem right there. He sank to the bottom of the lake floor. Unfortunately, he landed on the electrical box, which had electrical wires sticking out of it. Eddy found himself tangled in the wires and some became tied to his arms.

With that happening, a big bolt of electricity from one of the batteries came out of the box and it tossed Eddy and the electrical box up out of the water, into the air and then back into the canoe. Which now meant the lake was clean once more.

"Hooray. The lake is now clean and we didn't do anything to clean it up!" Benny the fish yelled happily.

Eddy woke up, recovering from the sudden shock that had been dealt to his body.

"Huh?" Eddy wondered.

All the fish were surprised that Eddy woke up so soon especially since Eddy had electricity flowing through his body from the explosion.

"Come on, Eddy. Get up and celebrate with us," Benny the fish called from the surface of the lake.

"Aw! Please mom just five more minutes," Eddy yawned, thinking he was still sleeping in his bed at home.

All the fish wondered why Eddy said that they were his mom. Benny the fish grabbed a long stick floating in the water and jabbed Eddy with it.

"What are you doing?" Eddy yelled.

"So he is still alive, fool!" the Mr. T Fish shouted.

Eddy wondered why the Mr. T Fish always said *fool* at the end of every sentence as he seemed to say it to everybody.

Eddy tried to get up but he couldn't because he was still too weak.

Another boat floated nearby, a man rowing as he sang a song.

"Oh! I'm dumping garbage in the lake. Even though it gets dirty, I don't care," the strong man in the boat sang.

He was so strong because he was carrying a four foot tall trash barrel with no cover on top of it. This was because it was so full of trash that the cover wouldn't fit.

"HEY! What are you doing!" Eddy screamed.

The strong man turned his head to look at Eddy.

"I'm going to get rid of this stuff," the strong man said.

Eddy's eyes creased in anger, his face turning red.

"Nobody is going to dump anything into this lake while I'm here. Especially not a poor excuse for a strong man like *you*!" Eddy shouted angry.

The strong man began to get frustrated with Eddy. So he started to pour the garbage into the lake.

"How do you like me now?" the strong man screamed.

Eddy dove into the water and swam like a dolphin towards the boat with the strong man on it. Luckily, Eddy got there in time to push his hands against the four foot tall trash barrel and to keep even one bit of garbage from touching the lake water. For some reason, Eddy gained amazing strength to be able to push the trash barrel back onto the strong man's side of the boat where it all fell on him, covering him from head to toe with banana peels and coffee grinds.

There was a little drop of garbage heading for the water but Eddy reached out and caught it one millimeter before it touched the water. The fish were almost blind with amazement when they saw what Eddy did to that poor excuse of a strong man.

"That was great!" Benny the fish shouted.

"Way to do a good job, fool," Mr. T fish said.

"Thanks, well I have to leave now. Bye."

All the fish waved bye, Eddy now their friend.

Eddy grabbed everything of his and started back home to return to his family.

Eddy had to skip through the woods to get back home.

Halfway there, he heard a rustling in the trees.

"Huh! Who's there?" Eddy questioned.

Something popped out from behind a tree.

"It's me, little Billy Jr.," a little baby squirrel said.

Eddy looked around but he didn't see anybody who could have said those words.

"I'm down here!" little Billy Jr. yelled in a squeaky voice.

Eddy looked down by his feet and then he saw a cute little baby squirrel.

"Hey, little guy. What's your name?" Eddy said.

Billy Jr. began to look angry because he already said his name and Eddy didn't listen.

"My name is Billy Jr.!" Little Billy Jr. shouted.

Eddy was surprised at the talking squirrel. I mean, talking fish was one thing, but squirrels? That was ridiculous.

"Ah! It talks!" Eddy screamed.

While Eddy was screaming, raccoons were attacking the squirrel's home in another tree and taking the squirrel's nuts for the winter.

"Everyone, get those nuts back!" Billy Sr. screamed. He was twice the size of Billy Jr. with a big bushy tail.

On the father's order all squirrels ran and jumped from tree to tree to get their nuts back. Eddy was confused about what the squirrels were doing and why it was so important to get the nuts back. He asked Billy Jr. that very question.

"It took us seven months to collect all of those nuts for the winter. So you see that we either have to get those nuts back or we won't have enough food for ourselves for the cold, damp and snowy winter," Billy Jr. explained.

Eddy now had all of the answers to all of the questions that he asked Billy Jr., except one question that hadn't been answered yet.

"Is there anyway that I can help?" Eddy asked.

Billy Jr. thought for a moment and then came up with something, his nose twitching happily.

"There is a way that you can help. All you have to do is to get the metal bat at the bottom of the creek and go over to raccoon territory and start destroying everything so that our troopers can get our nuts back from those stealing raccoons," Billy Jr. said.

Eddy agreed and left, now on his way to the bottom of the creek. But it wasn't going to be that easy. The first step was to get over the crocodile pit without getting eaten.

But that didn't end up being that hard. All Eddy did was wait until all of the alligator's mouths were closed and then he hopped on them before they opened their mouths again.

The second step was to use a vine to crawl over the quick sand and to get across by using the vine to keep from sinking. This was easy because Eddy had great upper body strength from doing push-ups every day.

The third step was to run away from the tied up vine ball and into the hole to get to the next step. Eddy was a fast runner because he jogged on his treadmill every day of the week. Then the fourth step was to tame three wild tigers with a whip. Eddy just kept on whipping them continuously until they ran away. The fifth step and the final step was to not eat chocolate with nuts which the squirrels had gathered together.

Eddy just adored chocolate and chocolate with nuts were his favorite. But he had to resist it because those were all of the squirrel's nuts that the raccoons would always take from them.

Luckily Eddy had some sugar in his pocket so he ate that instead, feeding his sweet tooth. Eddy finally came face to face with the metal bat. He grabbed it and for some weird reason it was pointing up to the sky.

He looked up to see yet another meteorite about to hit the forest in about three, two, one, zero!

The meteorite came crashing down and it destroyed everything in its path. It was a good thing that the raccoon's fortress was in the middle of the meteorite strike when it hit. All the raccoons ran away so as not to get killed by it.

"HOORAY! The raccoons are finally gone and we get all of our nuts back!" little Billy Jr. yelled. "I guess we didn't need your help after all."

"That's okay," Eddy said.

Eddy packed up his stuff and said his goodbyes.

"Please come again, Eddy. We'll miss you," little Billy Jr. said, waving with one small paw.

While Eddy was walking away, he raised his hand, making a goodbye sign. Little Billy Jr. almost cried because he wanted Eddy to stay with him. Soon, Eddy was gone from sight, lost in the woods again.

Next Eddy had to walk through a neighborhood to get home and there was a kid named Peter walking down the street.

"Hey, just so you know, there's been rumors about how a helicopter dropped some liquid into a power plant and a little bit of the stuff fell into a lake. Then a cat fell in, too, and some people now say its become a zombie cat," Peter said.

"Hey, kid. You should get out of the street," Eddy said to Peter.

"Why?" Peter asked.

Peter was soon about to find out why he had to get out of the street. There was a cat walking down the street right behind him. Peter turned around and looked at the cat. Eddy knew immediately there was something wrong with that cat. The cat's fur was all dirty and covered in dirt and blood, and its head looked like someone had stepped on it.

"Look out!" Eddy yelled.

With a howl of rage, the zombie cat prepared to bite off Peter's arm. Thinking fast, Eddy got a ball of yarn out of his bag and threw it into a nearby house. The ball went flying and broke a window to the left of the front door. The zombie cat jumped after the ball of twine and into the house.

But a woman had been in the house and she had picked up the twine, not understanding who would throw it at her house.

The zombie cat jumped up high and bit the woman's arm off to get the ball of yarn, its strong teeth chewing like a piranha's.

"Run, kid, run!" Eddy screamed to Peter.

"My name isn't kid, okay? It's Peter."

At that moment in time Eddy knew that Peter was a dumb kid. He should be running for his life, not worrying about if Eddy knew his name.

"I don't really care what your name is, just run!" Eddy yelled.

Peter looked mad.

"What do you mean, run? Why?" Peter asked.

Eddy didn't waste his breath talking to Peter because things had gone from bad to worse.

Now there were four zombie cats coming out of the house and they wanted some more meat in their zombie stomachs. Eddy never thought that he would come face to face with a zombie, let alone a bunch of zombie cats.

Now Eddy has to go over all the facts he knew about zombie cats.

Fact number one: They don't play with cat toys; they like to play with eyeballs. Fact number two: They don't eat cat food, they eat human guts.

Fact number three: They have noses ten times stronger than humans.

Fact number four: They are always two steps ahead of their prey.

Fact number five: There can be a king cat, queen cat, prince cat, and a princess cat.

Fact number six: Their bellies don't have any skin on them.

Fact number seven: They have fangs not teeth.

Fact number eight: They don't care about anybody but themselves.

Fact number nine: With their zombie eyes they can see up to ten miles.

Fact number ten: If they bite you then you turn into a zombie.

Eddy then ran for his life while Peter just stood there and got bit, the zombie cats sinking their fangs into his flesh.

"Aw, man. And this is a new shirt," Peter said as he fell to the grass and was eaten, piece by bloody piece. The zombie cats pulled out his intestines and chomped in his spleen. They ate his heart and fought over his kidneys, then played a game with his gallbladder. Soon Peter woke up as a zombie and wandered away, now looking for fresh humans to kill. Seeing Eddy running away, Peter headed for the woods, too.

While Peter was getting eaten, Eddy ran into the woods and climbed into the highest tree in the forest.

The zombie cats were finished with Peter in just a few minutes and followed Peter into the woods on Eddy's trail. While Eddy was in the tree, he found out that he'd scraped himself on a rock when he was running. Blood was dripping down his arm and onto the ground of the forest.

The zombie cats didn't know where Eddy was but the king cat smelled a barbecue going. The smell was coming from the east side of the forest and the zombie cats were on the west side of the forest. None of the cats knew their left and rights. Luckily, one of the cats had a better sense of direction. With this cat in the lead, they went east and they found a man yelling because there was a poisonous snake on the ground trying to bite him.

"Ooh, lunch," the queen cat hissed.

She tried to run and eat the man but the king zombie cat grabbed the queen cat's tail and pulled her back without the man noticing that there were zombie cats behind the short and bushy trees surrounding him.

"Ouch!" the queen cat yelled.

"Calm down, honey. All we need to do is to make up a hypothesis," the king cat said.

"What kind of hypothesis?" the queen cat asked.

"A good one. Anyone have one?" the king cat asked.

The princess cat raised her hand because she had a hypothesis and she thought it was a good one.

"How about we get a tree to squish him," the princess cat said.

The king cat nodded up and down and then gave his answer.

"It just might work," the king cat said.

One of the cats stole an axe from the screaming man and dragged it away. The king cat, with the help of two more cats, chopped down the tree. This was hard because their paws couldn't hold the axe handle but eventually they managed it.

As the tree began to fall, the queen cat jumped out and scared the screaming man right under the tree, and before they knew it the zombie cats were having the dead man for breakfast, lunch, and dinner.

"That was delicious," the queen cat said as she chewed on a piece of spleen.

"Okay. Now lets get back home everyone," the king zombie cat said.

He tried to get up but he couldn't because his belly was up to his forehead when he lay down, it was now so stuffed with human meat. He looked like a balloon that had been over inflated

"Can somebody help me up?" the king cat whined.

The princess cat couldn't lift the king cat up because she was too weak and full herself. So the princess cat and the prince cat together tried to lift the king cat. But both of them were weak also. Finally the princess cat, the prince cat, and the queen cat tried to lift the king cat up and they were strong enough. With the king cat up, all three of the other royal zombie cats fell down. Good thing the king cat was strong enough to lift all three of the royal zombie cats up off the ground.

The zombie cats headed home and on their way they passed right by where Eddy was hiding. But Eddy had fallen asleep hiding in the tree and without even thinking about it, Eddy fell out of the tree.

Before he hit the ground, the king cat said one thing.

"Hey, Eddy! We killed your family!" the king cat yelled.

Right after Eddy heard those words he grabbed a tree branch and he flipped it up, the tree bark flaking off.

"YOU DID WHAT!" Eddy screamed.

"You heard us," the king cat said. "We killed them and ate them all."

Eddy threw the branch at the cats and then dashed forward as he aimed for the king cat first with his right fist. But before Eddy hit the king cat, the princess cat got in between the king cat and Eddy. By accident, Eddy hit the princess cat, but then Eddy used his left foot to kick the king cat. When the king cat got hurt the rest of the zombie cats got hurt, too. Right there that gave Eddy his eleventh fact about zombie cats.

Fact number eleven: If the king cat gets hurt then in some weird way the other cats get hurt, too.

"How do you like me now? Huh!" Eddy screamed.

Eddy used every part of his body to kick and punch the king cat and all the other cats, beating up their bodies. Finally, every single zombie cat had died again. Eddy had avenged his family. Now he had nothing left. So he went back to the fishes and the squirrels. But they were all dead. Every single innocent soul killed. Even cute little Billy Jr. and Benny the fish. Even Mr. T Fish.

So all Eddy had left was vengeance.

He left the woods and went to his neighbor's house. He knew Mr. Miller had lost of weapons in an old shed in his back yard

As Eddy broke the lock on the door and entered the shed, his eyes went wide at what he saw.

"I'm one lucky guy," Eddy said.

There were loads of weapons on the walls and on shelves. Bazookas, sniper rifles, machine guns, pistols, and knives. You name it and it was there.

He picked up a bazooka and fired it, and the bazooka blew the roof off of the shed. Then he used a sniper rifle and it destroyed a trash barrel sitting on the sidewalk.

"That's gonna wake the neighbors," Eddy said.

Two grenades blew up a house outside and the machine guns made thousands of holes in the shed walls. The knife he knew was very sharp. Eddy came out looking like a G.I. Joe action figure, covered with weapons all over his small body.

"I will avenge my family. I swear I will," Eddy said.

When Eddy went back to the woods, he saw the zombie cats were gone. They weren't dead yet it seemed. Then he heard a noise behind him and when he turned around the zombie cats were there, only now they were bruised and battered from the beating Eddy had given them.

Marching towards the zombie cat's, Eddy raised his weapons.

"You looking for me?" Eddy asked.

"No, we're looking for a boy named Peter," the king cat said.

"But Peter is dead. He died when you ate him," Eddy said.

"And where would that be exactly?" the king cat asked.

"Why, Colorado of course," Eddy answered.

"Not that Peter, this Peter," the king cat said.

The king cat showed Eddy a picture of the Peter that they were looking for.

"Hey. I know him. He's my son," Eddy said. "But you said he was dead."

"Nope, we lied, he wasn't there. Where is he? Tell us!" the king cat screamed.

"He's probably at school right now," Eddy said.

"What school, where?" the king cat asked.

"The school is over there," Eddy pointed.

The school was across the street.

"Let's go, zombie cats," the king cat said.

"Yes, let's," the other cats said.

"Oh, no, you don't," Eddy said and tried to shoot the cats but they got away, moving fast.

The zombie cats went to the school and waited for Peter to leave, then they followed Peter home.

"We attack at midnight," the king cat whispered.

"Hooray," the other cats whispered loudly.

Peter put on his bathrobe and went straight to his bed. Peter heard laughing in the wind. He looked outside and saw the zombie cats.

"He's spotted us!" the queen cat yelled.

"Run!" the king cat screamed.

Peter got dressed and ran outside to chase after them, not understanding what was happening.

"Where're you going, honey," Peter's mother asked.

"Work," answered Peter, lying.

"Wow! So you finally got yourself a job," his mom said.

"Yeah, whatever," Peter said.

When Peter went outside it was freezing. Like below zero degrees Celsius. And it wasn't even the middle of winter. It was the beginning of the month of June. It was weird.

At the end of the street was a snowing machine that was spewing out snow. The driver was none other than the king cat and on the top of the machine the other cats were lined up, all with fangs that wanted to tear into him. Peter ran and ran but he couldn't out run the cats. He got on his bike and peddled to Mount Rushmore. He took a really tall ladder up to the top. The ride was short for some reason, like fifteen minutes. The ladder went right back down after it touched the top. The zombie cats got on the ladder and were now following Peter onto Mount Rushmore. It was a steep slope so Peter had to make sure he didn't fall off or else his body would splatter all around the rocks below and it would just be a huge mess.

Finally the zombie cats reached the top.

"You can't run from us forever," the king cat said.

"What do you want with me?" Peter asked. "I don't know you cats."

"You have a special brain that gives you good luck," the king cat said. "And we want to eat it so we'll have good luck too."

"Hmm. Good luck you say?" Peter said. "I didn't know that. But it would explain a lot of stuff that had happened in my life, like good grades and winning at the carnival."

"So hold still so we can eat you brains," the king cat said.

Not wanting to get his brains eaten, Peter jumped off Mount Rushmore.

"What, is he crazy?" the king cat said, surprised as Peter fell away all the way to the rocks below.

"Must be," the princess cat replied.

But Peter didn't die, he was so lucky he landed on a hot air balloon that was just filling up and floating by.

"Well. That was convenient," Peter said.

The zombie cats jumped also but the hot air balloon was out of reach and they missed it.

"Aw. Son of a biscuit!" the king cat whined as they all fell to the rocks below.

Their bodies were squished against the jagged rocks as if you had used a hammer to squish a rotten tomato.

The hot air balloon floated all the way back to his house and Peter slid off. With a weave the balloon floated away and Peter was alone.

The next morning, Peter was silently whistling a tune as he walked to school.

At school, he met his friend's John and Brian. And let's not forget his girlfriend Meg. As they talked in the cafeteria, a steam pipe broke and steam filled the air. Peter was talking to his friends when he saw the steam.

Peter warned his friends and his girlfriend. John and Brian listened to him, but Meg just kept putting her make-up on.

"Come on, Meg," Peter said. "We have to leave!"

"Hello, I can't leave yet. I'm putting my make-up on," Meg said.

Meg turned around only to see a shape in the whitish steam coming for her. Not knowing what to do, she sprayed her perfume at it and it transformed into a big, white, creepy, and weird smoke monster.

"Ahhhh! Help me!" Meg screamed. "A monster!"

The smoke monster grabbed Meg by the arm and put her on its steam-like shoulders.

"Why me?" Peter asked. "Coming, Meg," he yelled as he ran to save her.

But first he went to his locker to put his books away. If he just dropped and left them on the floor then someone might steal or take them and he'd get in trouble.

"Peter! Get over here and get me off of this freak!" Meg yelled.

Peter went to save Meg, but forgot to close his locker. Peter was obsessed with keeping things organized.

"Peter. I'm not going to say this again," Meg said. "Help me!"

Peter shut the locker and went to save Meg. She was already halfway down the hallway so Peter had to take a shortcut to catch her. He jumped on the stairs and dashed to the other side.

"Peter is that you?" Meg asked.

"Shhh! Yes, it's me. Now be quiet," Peter answered.

Peter jumped from the top stair and landed on the smoke monster.

And went right through it.

"What happened?" Peter wondered.

Peter wondered how Meg was staying on the monster's shoulder without falling through its steam-like body.

"Now. This is a real challenge for the best of the best," Peter said.

"Peter hit its stomach. It's the weak spot!" Meg yelled.

Peter slipped right between the smoke monster's legs and hit him in the stomach.

"Ouch!" screamed the hurt smoke monster.

There was a fire extinguisher behind Peter and he grabbed it, then sprayed it at the monster. The monster, made of steam, suddenly began to become frozen and when it was like ice, Peter used the bottom of the canister to crash it into the smoke monster's stomach. It shattered into a thousand pieces and Meg fell to the floor with a yelp.

"There, it's gone now," Peter said with a grin.

"You saved me, Peter, thank you," Meg said.

She hugged him and he let her and when she was done, they both headed back to the cafeteria. It was pizza today and he knew he didn't want to miss that.

*   *   *

"Peter, come on, honey, wake up, you'll be late for school," Peter's mother said as she shook him gently.

Peter opened his eyes. A moment ago he had been in school, after fighting a smoke monster. And then he had dreamed about his dad and how he had fought zombie cats.

"Wow, Mom, I had the weirdest dream, you wouldn't believe it if I told you."

"Maybe so, honey, but it's almost eight, you need to get dressed, brush your teeth and get to school."

"Yes, Mom," Peter said.

He got out of bed and did the things all kids do in the morning and as he left for school, he whistled a silent tune.

It had all been a dream, and wow, what a dream.

As he walked to school, he didn't see the zombie cat hiding in the bushes, its bloodied muzzle covered in gore as its beady eyes watched Peter intently.

Maybe it was a dream, but then again, maybe it wasn't.

ANTHONY GIANGREGORIO

LOST IN THE WOODS
A WEREWOLF TALE

"**W**e're lost, aren't we?" Sharon said from the passenger seat as she stared at the map spread out before her.

"No, we're not," Thomas replied as he steered the car around a sharp bend in the road.

Over two hours had passed now since the road had changed from asphalt to gravel, and then to dirt. The rains had carved deep grooves into the road, causing the car to jump on its shocks, like Thomas had decided to take them offroading.

"We need to turn around," Sharon said as she tossed the map into the back seat where their camping supplies were. Only the sleeping bags and their tent were in the trunk. "*You* need to turn around," she said again as she stared out through the front windshield at the woods.

Though the sun was high in the sky, the tree tops stopped more than half the light from penetrating. Because of this it seemed almost like twilight, only a few thin rays cutting though the holes in the leafy canopy. Birdcalls could be heard over the sound of the car's engine and sometimes deer could be spotted grazing off in the distance, between the wooded glades they drove past.

"We can't turn around, dear," Thomas said, saying the word *dear* sarcastically. "There's no place I can manage it. The damn trees grow right up to the edge of the road and even if I still tried the shoulder's muddy. This isn't a truck you know, we'll get stuck."

"Oh, is that what you call what we're on, a road?" she added in a sarcastic tone of her own.

He glanced away from the road long enough to stare her down.

"Be nice, this isn't my fault," he said calmly.

She had been prepared to snap at him, expecting him to do the same, but when he ended up talking calmly it threw her off.

"Oh, I...I know that, Thomas, it's just, we're getting deeper into the woods, who knows what's out there. We need to turn back. What if we break down?"

He nodded at her words, taking them in.

"Yeah, I was thinking the same thing." He pointed to his cell phone on the dashboard, the cord to the cigarette lighter keeping it charged. "Check that will you? Do we even have a signal out here?"

She did as he asked and a second later shook her head. "Nope, no signal."

"Shit, that was what I was afraid of." He shrugged slightly. "Look, Sharon, this road has to go somewhere. All we need to do is follow it until I can find someplace safe enough to spin around."

"This was a mistake," she said as she wrapped her arms around herself protectively. "We shouldn't have come out here. We're city people, camping isn't our thing."

"Oh, please," he said. "I used to go camping all the time when I was a kid."

"Yes, you did, but that was with your father when you were eleven. He did everything, you didn't have to do a thing."

"Maybe, but I still remember enough so we can have some fun."

"Not anymore, we must be miles from the campsite by now."

"No, dear, more than that. We've been driving for hours, I'd say twenty miles easy."

She turned to him, then, her eyes grew wide. "You mean to tell me we're more than twenty miles deep into the woods?"

"So what?" he chuckled as he swung around another dip in the road. "Come on, Sharon, this isn't the movies, there's no man with a leather mask and a chainsaw or inbred hillbillies who want to eat us for lunch out here. That's just the stuff of Hollywood. We're perfectly safe."

She shook her head, her brown tresses caressing her cheeks. "I don't know, Thomas. We haven't seen any signs of civilization for hours. For all we know we're the only ones out here."

"Yeah, maybe," he replied and concentrated on the road.

With the car jumping and bucking like a wild bronco, they drove deeper into the dense forest.

*   *   *

"You know, it's funny..." Thomas said as he fought the wheel as the car bounced over yet another bad dip.

Sharon waited for him to continue and when he didn't she frowned.

"What's funny?" she prodded.

He shrugged slightly, something he was wont to do when he was considering something.

"Well, it's just we're so far in the woods now, you know? I mean, this is the kind of place you'd find Bigfoot skulking around between the trees."

"Bigfoot? Oh, Thomas, don't be silly. Besides, Bigfoot has sightings only in the Northeast, we're in the west."

He looked at her, his left eyebrow coming up in curiosity.

"And how in the world do you even know that?"

She shrugged herself, brushing her hair from her face. "I just do. I read and watch TV too, you know."

He reached out and cupped her chin in his hand, rubbing her cheek with his thumb. It was times like this when he was reminded of just how much he loved the woman sitting next to him. It was when she showed something about herself he didn't know was there. Even after almost twelve years of marriage she could still surprise him.

It was as he was looking at her, his eyes off the road, that the right front tire found a deeper, wider pothole than most of the ones Thomas had been dealing with. Without warning, the car's front tire plummeted into the pothole, the vehicle coming to a halt so hard and fast both of them were thrown forward. Neither was wearing a seatbelt, deciding in the middle of nowhere it wasn't needed. And with the new laws demanding they wear one in the city, they both felt like little rebels by unbuckling them as soon as they hit the mountain pass.

But now those lack of seatbelts was a detraction as both of them were tossed around the car like rag dolls.

Sharon's head struck the windshield and she was lifted a foot off her seat and Thomas cried out as the steering wheel dug deep into his upper chest. He felt sudden pain shoot through his body and his mind told him he'd probably cracked a rib or two.

The car lurched forward like a torpedoed ship, the rear end coming up off the road slightly from the momentum. But then it rocked back to earth as the two passengers were slammed back against their seats. There was a small blood spot on the windshield where Sharon's head had connected with the glass; her body now slumped forward in her seat, unconscious.

Thomas sucked in a breath of air, trying to fight the pain in his chest, but his body went into shock, and before he could stop himself, he felt the world going dark. He reached out and tried to touch Sharon, wanting to see if she was all right, but before he could, his arm dropped to the seat and he slipped into oblivion.

*   *   *

There was a tapping sound filling his dream as Thomas finally came back to wakefulness.

For a brief second he thought he was blind. His eyes were open but he couldn't see a thing. Looking left and right, he heard the tapping growing louder now. It was coming from above him and as he reached out and felt the switch for the window, he pressed the button, the window rolling down.

Immediately he was splashed with water and he realized the noise was rain hitting the roof and hood of his car so he raised the window.

The car had stalled and he looked to the dash and could see the dim glow of the numbers and letters. Reaching out, he turned on the dome light and was blinded by the glare until his eyes could focus again.

And then he gasped in shock to see Sharon slumped in her seat, her head resting against the passenger window.

"Oh my God, Sharon? Are you all right?" he asked as he leaned over and pulled her to him. She groaned slightly and he thanked God she was alive. He felt her head, and when his hand came away with blood on it, he gasped again. When he inspected her scalp, he found the small cut on the top of her forehead where her head had whacked the windshield.

She groaned again and then her eyes fluttered open.

"Ohhhh, what happened?"

"I don't know, I think we crashed," Thomas said.

"Crashed? We were in the middle of a deserted road. How on God's green Earth did you manage that one?"

"Like I just said, I don't know. Are you hurt? I mean, other than that cut on your head?"

She took stock of herself, groaning as she sat up, but after a minute she felt she was fine, only a splitting headache the result of the crash.

"I'm fine, just a headache. You?"

Thomas nodded in the glow of the dome light. "My chest hurts a little, but I'll live."

She smiled slightly. "Want me to kiss the boo-boo and make it all better?"

"Ha, ha, I really don't think now is the time for that," he joked as he shifted in his seat.

He put the car into park, the engine having stalled, and now he turned it over, the motor starting right up, but as he tried to move the car it wouldn't budge. He could feel the engine wanting to push the car along but the vehicle felt like it was dragging or like it had a flat. He knew there was only one thing to do.

Turning off the engine, but leaving the headlights on, he reached into the backseat for his jacket and a flashlight as Sharon watched silently. She rubbed at her window, the condensation coming away, but she couldn't see a thing. It was pitch black outside on the road and the surrounding woods.

"How long was I out?" she said to herself, but Thomas thought she was speaking to him.

"Don't know, a few hours I guess. I was out, too. We both took a beating. Guess that's what we get for not wearing our seatbelts."

Her reply was a soft grunt. She didn't need a lecture now about auto safety.

He opened his door and was about to get out when she grabbed his arm.

"Wait, where're you going?"

"I have to see what's wrong with the car, Sharon."

"But it's raining out, you'll get soaked."

He grinned at her. "Sharon, it's only rain, I'll be fine. Now you stay here and try to rest, I'll be right back."

"You be careful," she told him and he nodded while pushing the door open and stepping out.

As soon as his foot came down, it was swallowed by a six inch puddle and he felt the cold water seep into his hiking boot. Cursing silently, he ignored it and slammed the door closed to keep the inside of the car dry. Then he turned on the flashlight and shrugged into his jacket, all the while moving to the front of the car. The headlights barely helped push back the night, the rain and fog from the moisture in the air bringing visibility down to nothing. But he managed to make it to the front bumper without falling on his face. Once there, he flashed the light on the tires, and after checking the left side and seeing all was well, he checked the right tire.

But what he'd hoped for, namely a flat, wasn't to be. The entire tire and rim was bent outward from the bottom, and when he got down on one wet knee and inspected it more, his head an inch from the muddy water that had filled the pothole, he saw that something had snapped behind the tire. Without a better inspection he guessed it was a tie rod or a ball joint, but in the end it didn't really matter.

The bottom line was they were screwed with a capital S.

Climbing to his feet and leaning on the hood, he looked out into the penetrating darkness.

And it was then he spotted a small twinkle of light coming from the south.

He stared at it for a few seconds, wondering if he'd imagined it, but as he watched longer the light didn't move.

He took a few steps to the side of the road, his eyes never leaving the light, and when it didn't disappear he felt confident he'd found something.

But then the light blinked out like it was never there to begin with.

But Thomas knew what he'd seen. The light hadn't been his imagination. A light had been on and then turned off. But it looked far away, a mile at least. He knew light would travel in the darkness of the woods, and sometimes things that appeared close were miles away.

Must be a ranger station or something this far out in the woods. What else could it be? he thought.

He decided he had two choices. He and Sharon could sit in the car until Hell froze over as the chances of someone else coming down this abandoned road was one in a million. Or they could head out towards where he'd seen the light and hope for the best.

It took him all of a minute of standing in the rain to make his decision. Turning, he moved back to the car and opened the door, then climbed inside. Sharon flinched away from him, not wanting to get wet. He found it ironic she did this as in a minute or two she would be as soaked as him, she just didn't know it yet.

He turned to her and stared into her eyes. Not saying a word. She waited silently, and when he didn't speak, she prompted him with a question.

"Well? Is the car okay?"

"No, Sharon, it's not. It's not going anywhere. But we are."

"What're you talking about?" she asked.

He shook his head. "Don't worry about that now, I'll tell you on the way."

"On the way? To where?"

"I saw a light to the south of here. It has to be a rescue station or ranger station or something."

"And?" she inquired.

"And we're going there. So get your stuff, were going on a hike."

"In this rain? Are you crazy?"

He smiled then, the water running down his cheeks, his matted wet hair making him look like a school boy. "Maybe, but now's as good a time as any, so let's go. I'll go without you if I have to if you don't mind being all alone in the middle of nowhere."

Not waiting for an answer, he opened his door and stepped out, closing the door again. He knew she would never stay alone and by pretending to leave her he would save precious time not arguing.

"Thomas? Don't leave without me, Thomas?" But he wasn't listening as he began trudging to the edge of the road.

"Oh, and don't forget our gear!" he called out with a slight grin, knowing she would be right along behind him.

"Ohhhh, you jerk," she mumbled.

She knew what he was doing. She wouldn't stay alone, he knew she would come, and by leaving the car he stopped her from complaining and trying to talk him out of it. She knew all his tricks, but she also knew this one would work on her.

Feeling outmaneuvered and hating him for it, she reached in back and got her jacket and their backpacks, then opened her door.

As she stood up, slamming the door behind her. Thomas flashed her a smile, the flashlight illuminating his face.

"You ready?"

"As if I have a choice," she pouted.

"Exactly," he said, then turned and moved off, Sharon running around the car to catch up.

As she reached him, he slowed and she handed him his pack.

Then he reached out and took her hand, and though wet and cold from the falling rain, she gripped it tight, the two moving off into the woods in the direction Thomas had seen the light.

*   *   *

"That doesn't look like a ranger's station," Sharon said blandly as they slowed down to rest under a tree. The rain was so heavy even with the thick canopy above, the rain found its way through. Only now the water dripped off leaves, the droplets thicker as they struck the ground and them.

"Yeah, you're right, it's not," Thomas replied as he studied the ramshackle structure fifty feet in front of them.

Through the few trees, he could see the small shack had been built hastily or by someone without much skill as a carpenter. On top of logs that were obviously found scattered about the forest floor, after lightning strikes, there was a mishmash of man made wood mixed in as well. Old pieces of plywood and two by fours made up the framework of the small...well, it had to be called a cabin, but just barely.

"What should we do?" she asked as she wiped her brow with a soggy sleeve.

They were both soaked to the bone, having been walking for over an hour.

"Not much choice really. We go see if anyone's home." He set off then, carefully making his way over the soggy deadfall. "I know I saw a light on earlier, that's why I knew where to go. Someone's got to be inside."

"I doubt they're going to want visitors, Thomas. Especially if they live way out here in the middle of nowhere."

He shrugged, the gesture lost in the darkness.

"It's probably just some hermit or survivalist who's preparing for the end of the world."

"If it is he could have a gun, Thomas," she stated nervously.

"Oh, please, you're letting your imagination run away with you again. We'll be fine."

Crossing the remaining distance, they stopped when they were only a few feet away from the cabin. Now that they were closer, they could see moss growing on the sides and actual tree branches jutting out of the foundation. It looked like it was fifty years old and only the debris mixed in with the walls told it wasn't that old. Thomas stepped up to the door and to the right he saw soda cans and glass bottles mixed with mud lathered on the outer shell of the cabin. When he reached out and touched it, the mud felt hard, though some did come off on his fingertips. He had a feeling whoever lived here must have to constantly keep up on the walls or the rain would end up washing it all away.

With a glance to Sharon, Thomas knocked on the door. He rapped three times and waited, and when no one answered, he knocked harder, and this time the door opened a little.

Only an inch, the door dragged along the floor and Thomas pushed it open some more, stepping inside.

"Wait, Thomas, don't go in there," Sharon whispered.

"Why not?" Thomas called over his shoulder. "I didn't come all this way to leave 'cause no one's home. Come on in and get out of the rain," he called as he disappeared into the darkness of the cabin.

"But why wasn't it locked?"

"There's no one around for miles and miles, what would be the point?" he called from the darkness, now come on in and quit being a baby."

Sharon stood at the doorway for all of ten seconds, then she looked behind her at the dark forest, gazed up at the full moon hidden behind the clouds, and entered the cabin, not wanting to be left alone. She closed the door behind her to keep out the rain.

As she entered, her nose scrunched up in disgust at the charnel house smell permeating the cabin.

"Oh my God, what's that smell?" she gasped. "Thomas, where are you?" she called as she stood near the door, not wanting to go in further.

"I'm over here," he said and then the flashlight was on and he was pointing the tight beam at her face.

"Get that damn thing out of my face, please," she growled angrily.

"Huh? Oh, sorry, honey, wasn't thinking." Thomas dropped the light and then played it across the cabin's surfaces, the circular beam roving over the walls and a table in the corner. It was a one room structure with a bed in the corner and a closet at the opposite end. A sink and table was set up in the other corner and a small, homemade couch was in the middle. A smaller table was next to the couch and a few well read books and magazines lay strewn on its surface. Thomas went to these first and picked one up.

"It's over ten years old," he said.

Sharon was still looking around in the gloom of the only flashlight and she spotted something over by the sink and table.

"What's that over there?"

Thomas dropped the *People* magazine and turned, flashing the beam where she wanted.

"I don't know," he said as he moved closer. It was when he was right over it that the light brought it into focus and he gasped in surprise. Then he felt his stomach churning and he leaned over the sink and expelled his earlier lunch of tacos and beer.

"Thomas? What's wrong? Are you all right?"

Thomas wasn't listening as he vomited into the sink. When his stomach was empty, he sighed and wiped his mouth with the back of his soggy jacket.

Sharon began to cross the cabin towards him and he raised his hand to stop her.

"You don't want to see this," he said as he caught his breath.

"Don't tell me what I do and don't want to see, Thomas, I'm not a child," she snapped as she stepped closer and glazed down at what had freaked Thomas out.

"Oh, my God. Is that?"

"Yeah, I think it is," he replied.

But Sharon appeared to be made of sterner stuff and her stomach stayed calm as she leaned over and studied the thing on the table. There was a small stick to the side and she used it to pick up the thing, and as Thomas flashed the light on it, she nodded.

"Good God, Thomas, this is human skin."

"It can't be, that's crazy. You're mistaken," he said even though he thought this too and that's why he'd vomited.

She shook her head and then slowly turned what looked like a dried piece of pale leather so he could see the other side. "Then what do you call this?"

Thomas looked where she pointed and saw a tattoo of a heart with an arrow and the name Cheryl in the middle. The tattoo was faded, the owner probably getting it years ago, and as he stared at it, he felt his stomach building up like Old Faithful and he turned and spewed into the sink again.

Sharon ignored him and set the disgusting thing down. Though gross, this still didn't explain the smell of rancid meat she'd detected upon entering the cabin. Now that she'd been in here for a bit, it wasn't as bad, but she could still detect it.

"Here, tough guy, give me that light," she said.

Thomas handed it to her and she used it to search the corner some more. There was a small cabinet with a single door and she opened it.

As the door opened, the smell of putrid, rotting meat wafted into her face and she jumped back, kicking the door closed. It was as the door slammed shut that she was able to glimpse the shelves were full of meat; maggots and flies crawling along the ridges and valleys of the tissue. After seeing the skin, she didn't want to think about what kind of meat could be in there.

"Thomas, we need to leave here right now," she said.

"No argument from me," he replied and grabbed her by the arm as they headed for the door.

But as Thomas reached out to grab the doorknob, they both heard the sounds of footsteps as someone banged their feet on the side of the cabin to clean off the mud picked up while walking in the rain.

"Oh, shit, someone's here," he squeaked.

"What'll we do?" she asked, her eyes wide.

Thomas turned and looked about the cabin, searching for a way out, but there was none. There was the one window next to the only door, probably the one that light had bled through, but the rest of the cabin was solid walls. But then his eyes landed on the closet in the corner, and without asking, he ran to it, pulling her along with him.

"Quick, the closet, we can hide in there and sneak off whenever they leave again."

"But we don't know when that'll be," she protested.

He stopped at the closet and turned on her. "Do you have a better idea?" he hissed, his face manic with fear. Whoever was out there had human skin on his kitchen table. He didn't want to meet that person if he had a choice.

"No, I..."

"Then come on and shut up," he said, rushing into the closet and closing the door with her next to him, just as the outer door to the cabin opened.

Thomas kept the closet door slightly cracked so he could see into the cabin, and he prayed whoever was coming in didn't need anything or want to hang something up in the closet.

At first he couldn't see a thing. With the flashlight doused the cabin was pitch black, but the figure of a man moved about without light, knowing his home well.

A second later an oil lantern flickered to life and cast a pallid glow through the small interior. Thomas stared at the man, who was soaked to the bone, wearing a raincoat and rubber boots.

At first he looked like something out of a slasher flick, but then he pushed the hood of the coat off his head and Thomas saw the man was as ordinary as himself.

Thomas whispered to Sharon that it was just a man, and only one at that.

The man shrugged out of his jacket and kicked off his boots, letting them fall anywhere in the cabin.

In his left hand he carried two skinned rabbits, and he went to the kitchen and tossed them next to the human skin. If the man noticed the skin wasn't where he'd left it, he gave no sign.

Thomas cursed Sharon for her sloppiness for when she'd set the skin back down on the table. The man poured some water into a bowl and began washing the rabbits, for all the world his actions as mundane as could be.

"What's he doing?" Sharon asked from behind Thomas. She couldn't see what was happening.

"Nothing. He's got some rabbits and it looks like he's getting them ready to cook."

"What are we gonna do?" she whispered.

"We stay here," he whispered back. "Sooner or later we can sneak out. Maybe when he falls asleep."

She nodded, and he felt her chin brush his shoulder, then he went back to watching the man prepare his dinner.

As Thomas watched, he couldn't understand what the deal was with the human skin. This man didn't look like a killer, or a psycho, but if not, then why would there be human skin in the cabin?

The man went about his business, cooking the rabbits in oil, eating, then when he was through, he went to the homemade couch and plopped down and picked up a magazine while his left pinky poked at his teeth where a piece of meat had become lodged.

Thomas' stomach was rumbling now, the smell of the cooked rabbit hanging in the air. As he'd watched the man eat, he wanted nothing more than to jump out and introduce himself, then hope he could get some of that rabbit.

Behind him, Sharon had dozed off, and he could hear her breathing softly. The fact she was sleeping while standing up told him how truly exhausted she was.

The man read magazines for more than an hour and a half, and as Thomas' eyes grew heavy and he too wanted to sleep, the man finally stirred. He checked his wrist watch to see the time and then did something Thomas wasn't expecting.

He stripped off his clothes until he was standing in the nude. He was a hairy male specimen, with dark black hairs covering his chest and back.

As the man turned to his side, Thomas's eyes went wide at the sight of the same tattoo on the man's arm as the one on the skin on the table. That didn't make one bit of sense, but Thomas, now awake again, watched the man kick his clothing to the side and stretch out on the couch to go to sleep.

Feeling slightly uncomfortable, like a pervert peeking into his neighbor's windows, Thomas looked away then by pulling his eye away from the crack in the door. He stared at the inside of the door, listening to Sharon's breathing behind him and tried to get comfortable for a long night in the closet.

Fifteen minutes after the man in the cabin had stripped, Thomas could hear him snoring loudly and Thomas knew it was going to be along night. Checking his own wrist watch, the dials luminous, he saw it was just about midnight and he was surprised at how many hours he and Sharon had already been trapped inside the closet. And then he felt pressure on his bladder and realized he needed to pee.

Oh great, he thought, *if things aren't already bad enough.*

With nothing to do about it now, he leaned against the side of the closet and tried to get some sleep, envious of Sharon, already lost in slumber.

Three hours later a loud screaming filled the cabin, snapping Thomas awake. Sharon, behind him, also came awake and both were paralyzed with fear as they hid in the closet.

"Oh my God, Thomas, what's going on?"

"I don't, know, Sharon, shhhh, he'll hear you," Thomas said as he wiped drool from the side of his mouth and leaned towards the still open door. He'd been sleeping hard, evidently as exhausted as Sharon.

As his right eye lined up with the vertical crack of the door, he peered into the interior of the cabin and his mouth slowly began to fall open in utter disbelief.

"What's happening?" came Sharon's voice. She could hear the screaming and she was scared to death. Her hands were now wrapped around Thomas' forearms and he could feel her shaking. He couldn't blame her. What he was witnessing inside the cabin was the stuff of nightmares, of fairytales.

For just a second, he wondered if he was dreaming and he squeezed his eyes shut and willed himself to wake up, but when this didn't happen and his bladder announced he still needed to pee, he knew he was awake. He'd never had to go pee in a dream before.

More screams filled the cabin and Sharon pushed closer to him so her face was buried in his back. Though they had been inside, out of the rain, for hours, their clothes were still damp and the funky smell of wet wool came to his nose. His skin was cold and clammy and felt itchy in a few places he couldn't scratch at the moment. But then another bellow of pain filled the cabin and he focused on the crack, where the door met the frame.

The naked man who had fallen asleep on the couch wasn't exactly a man any longer. Thomas watched in horror as the man now rolled across the floor, his face twisted into a mask of utter agony.

But that wasn't what was so off-putting. It was what was happening to him.

As the man rolled about on the floor, his skin began to move, undulate, and bones began to shift and stretch. Pieces of skin, not able to stretch with the new shape his body was twisting into, were splitting and falling off to land sloppily on the floor. Where the pink skin once was, red muscle glistened in the light of the oil lantern, and as Thomas watched in abject horror, hair follicles appeared, slowly growing out of the scarlet tendons to coat the body. The hands and lower legs began to stretch, inches added to the length, and fingernails grew more than four inches. The face was the most frightening to Thomas. As he stared in fascination and fear, the cheekbones receded and the jaw extended, teeth inverting and popping out as others came in. Incisors grew to points and hair began to cover the entire face until the man's visage was gone, replaced by some creature of myths.

Like a fetus emerging from the womb, the man curled into a tight ball as he endured this transformation, but eventually he calmed and stretched, like a human waking after a night's sleep to yawn and stretch tired limbs.

With the molting skin of the man strewn across the floor like dirty laundry, the beast came to its knees and then stood. Its ankles were now at right angles, the creature standing on the tips of its toes, looking like it could pounce in an instant, its thigh muscles looking powerful, cords of muscle flexing under the dark, black fur.

Thomas couldn't believe it, but he couldn't doubt his eyes.

He was staring at an honest to God werewolf.

The werewolf raised its head to the ceiling and roared in what Thomas assumed was pleasure. The creature had broken loose of its human shell and was now free to roam the land.

But what Thomas hoped might happen, namely that the werewolf would leave the cabin to dash through the forest, didn't happen.

Instead, the werewolf, with its new heightened sense of smell, slowly began flicking its head back and forth as it looked about the cabin.

It took Thomas a second to realize what was happening, and when it did, he felt his bladder let go and urine roll down his pant leg.

The beast was getting the scent of him and Sharon. It knew something was added to the redolence of its home. He knew they were hiding in its lair!

No sooner did he think this then the werewolf spun on its feet, its black eyes staring directly at the closet.

Faster than Thomas could see, the creature lunged for the door and swiped at it, its long, four inch claws slicing through the wooden door like it was paper.

He screamed then, as did Sharon, the darkness of the closet and the cacophony of the werewolf attacking the door sounding like a train had fallen in with them. But then the werewolf locked the door in its paws and ripped it off its hinges, exposing Thomas and Sharon to it.

The door was ripped away like it had been caught in a hurricane and Thomas and Sharon found themselves staring up at the gaping maw of this mythical beast of legend. The creature had over a foot on Thomas, the seven foot stature making it look even more threatening, not that the teeth and claws didn't do the job nicely.

Absolutely locked in panic, Thomas turned into a coward and forgot about Sharon, only wanting to escape this nightmare vision. Dropping to the floor, he crawled between the legs of the werewolf and the creature looked down to see Thomas' butt disappear behind it. But then Sharon screamed and the werewolf's attention became riveted on her.

As Thomas scurried into a corner of the cabin, Sharon shrieked as she was grabbed by paws as large as her head and dragged out of the closet.

Thomas, now in a corner, watched in horror as Sharon was picked up, her feet dangling more than a foot off the floor.

"Oh, God, no, Sharon!" he screamed, realizing what he'd done. He'd left his wife at the mercy of the beast. True, if he'd stayed he would only have been taken first, but still, she was his wife, he should have died trying to save her.

But it was too late to take back his cowardice now. He could only watch in shock and terror as the werewolf raised its right paw with claws extended, the other holding Sharon by her head like a basketball, and swipe at her abdomen with those razor-sharp claws.

Sharon's screams abruptly stopped as her lower torso became warm, first blood spilling out, then her lower intestines. They poured out of her abdomen like boiled spoiled sausage from an over packed grocery bag cut at the bottom, and when they hit the floor, they splattered blood and gore in every direction.

Sharon's voice was locked in her throat as her mouth opened and closed like a landed fish. Thomas could only stare in shock, his left hand held out to her, but he was too petrified to move.

But the werewolf wasn't done with the invaders to its domain and as Sharon's mouth fluttered up and down, the beast raised its now bloody claw over its head and sliced her from neck to groin, opening her up like a boned fish.

Her ribcage was sliced in twain from the claws and her heart could be seen beating within, the steady beat fueled by her fear. The werewolf reached in, wrapped its claws around the pumping heart, and yanked it free in a bloody geyser that struck the rafters of the ceiling. Sharon's eyes went wide in pain and then her twitching limbs sagged, her body now resembling a rag doll.

The werewolf tossed the heart away and then shook Sharon, not understanding why she wasn't moving. Like a disgruntled child annoyed that its toy wouldn't work, it tossed her away to land in a heap of limbs in a corner. As the fresh corpse landed, the cracked ribcage allowed organs to spill out, a bloody pool of plasma spreading wide as the insides seeped out like soiled porridge.

Tom squeaked in disbelief. This couldn't be happening! It was all a lie. There was no way in hell his wife had just been gutted by a werewolf and now the beast was turning towards him, licking its claws with a long pink tongue as it breathed in and out like massive dog panting after a jog with its owner.

The werewolf dropped to all fours then, and began moving in a circle towards Thomas.

Now it was his turn.

If his bladder wasn't empty he knew he would have pissed himself again as he gazed at those dark black eyes with absolutely no mercy in them.

Knowing if he didn't move he was dead, Thomas forced his frozen legs to let him move and he shifted across the floor, sliding very slowly. The werewolf raised its hackles and Thomas could see it was about to attack, similar to when a guard dog is ready to pounce or a cat is about to leap on a play toy, its back legs seeming to wiggle from side to side.

Thomas could see instinctively he had less than a second to do something, anything, to save himself, and as the werewolf leaped, he reached up to the table where the rabbits had been prepared and managed to wrap his left hand around the hilt of the skinning knife lying amidst the offal and flesh of the leftover pieces of rabbit.

As his palm felt the cool hilt, the werewolf leaped, flying through the air and striking Thomas in the chest. Both went flying across the cabin to roll around and Thomas fought for his life to keep those sharp teeth and claws away from him.

But he was only human, battling something *more than* human, and he knew in the end he would loose. He felt claws bite into his hip, then another one slice into his right arm, then he felt teeth sink into his right shoulder.

Turning his head as he screamed, he found himself staring into the right eye of the beast as its jaw clamped down tight on his shoulder blade.

Thomas didn't know how he kept his head then. Maybe the pain he felt brought focus to his dazed mind, but as he turned, screaming as he stared back into the dark orb, he realized he'd found his chance, his one opening, to come out of this battle the victor.

As the pointed teeth sank deeper into his shoulder, he swung the skinning knife up and around and stabbed it into the right eye of the beast. The tip was sharp and it plunged into the eye like the orb was a black egg, continuing deeper into the brain. The full six inches of the blade slid into the socket, until the hilt began to grind on bone.

The werewolf's teeth receded and it railed backwards, its paws going to its damaged eye.

But it was too late to prevent its demise. As the creature howled in agony, its legs grew weak and with a mighty *huff*, it dropped face first onto the floor. Its claws carved long grooves into the wooden floor as it spasmed, but in seconds they ceased and the body tensed, then relaxed.

Thomas brought his left hand to his shoulder wound and pressed his palm to it to staunch the flow, then he sat perfectly still, too frightened to move, too terrified of what might happen if he did.

Eventually morning came, and as the sun touched the treetops and a dull gloom suffused the cabin through its one window, the werewolf slowly changed back to the man it once was.

Thomas watched the transformation with dull eyes, the impossible not as exciting as the night before, back when his wife was alive.

An hour after the beast had reverted back to a man, Thomas finally made himself move.

Crawling to the corpse, he used his boot to push the head, ready to crawl away if the dead man moved. But the man was dead, the hilt of the skinning knife still protruding out of the eye socket.

Still wanting a weapon, not feeling safe without one, Thomas went and with clouded eyes, wrapped a hand around the hilt of the knife and pulled it free. With a sucking sound it popped out and Thomas held it in front of him, ready for what might come next.

But nothing came next and he waited another panic-filled hour. He kept his attention away from Sharon's body lying only a few feet from him. Every time he glanced at her face, her open eyes accused him of leaving her.

Tears fuelled his eyes and clouded his vision and he let the tears flow, weeping over his lost mate and what he'd suffered. When he had the strength to stand, he did so, even to the point of washing up in a bowl near the sink.

As he did this, he washed the skinning knife clean, too, not wanting to get blood on his hands after washing up, and he read the small words etched on the side of the blade, near the hilt.

STERLING SILVER it said in fancy script.

"Well, I'll be, that shit's really true, too," he said as he stared down at the corpse of the man.

After bandaging his wounds, all but the bite to his shoulder not serious, he rested and tried to deal with his situation. His shoulder wound was bad, the punctures deep. He would need stitches, but for the moment all he could do was rip a sheet and use it to wrap the wound. It hurt like hell when he moved his right arm, but it couldn't be helped. He did find some aspirin which he popped greedily and then found a bottle of Vodka which he used to swallow the pills and deaden his senses.

The booze helped a lot when it came time to bury the bodies.

Knowing he could never explain any of what happened in the cabin to the authorities, he waited until he was strong enough and then dragged each of the bodies out of the cabin and through the woods a ways until he found a nice glade still within site of the cabin.

Then he buried his wife and the man who had killed her. The man got no marker on his grave, Thomas didn't care about him, but for his wife he cobbled together some stones. Then he made a cross out of branches, using some dried weeds to tie it together. It would do for now, he could do more later if he wanted when he was feeling better.

His morose task finished, he went back to the cabin, and though there was blood everywhere, on the floor and walls, he fell to the makeshift couch and passed out. When he awoke hours later, he drank the rest of the Vodka and fell back into oblivion.

He awoke that night, as the full moon touched the sky, and began screaming in agony, mimicking the previous owner's cries of pain. It felt like his insides were being ripped out with invisible hands.

Falling to the floor, he writhed in pain, and just before he passed out, the agony too much to bear, he saw hair follicles begin to grown on his arms as his nails grew an inch. Then, mercifully, he passed out, the conscious human mind not able to withstand the transformation he was about to succumb to.

*   *   *

The next morning, he opened his eyes to find himself on the ground outside the cabin. He was naked, his feet covered in mud, and his skin felt tingly. As he sat up, he found he had no hangover which was good. Standing up, he realized he hadn't felt this good physically in along time, though mentally he was in utter anguish over the death of Sharon. It was still so hard to believe and he wondered if it was all some acid-induced dream. Maybe he'd eaten some bad mushrooms found on the forest floor.

As he glanced down at his naked frame, he saw the places where he'd been clawed the previous day were gone now, and as he checked his shoulder wound, he found nothing there but the slightest hint of a scar.

Somehow he had healed over night.

Entering the cabin, he found more skin on the floor, this layer added to the one the man had shed when Tom had watched him change from inside the closet.

As he inspected it with his foot, he saw some of the skin had the same claw marks and slices he'd suffered, and he knew without a doubt this skin had been his.

And like a runaway freight train it hit him hard and fast, the realization of his fate sending him to his knees.

Though the original owner of the cabin was gone, there was now someone new to replace him.

And what else could he do? If he went home to the city, to his old life, there would be questions about how he went camping and didn't come back with his wife. And what about the curse? If he went home and then changed, he would only infect others upon biting them, and he knew this deep down in his gut, it was what the beast would do if other humans were around. It was its nature.

No, he wasn't an evil man, he wouldn't bring this curse back to the civilized world.

And then he knew why the first man had lived here like a hermit, locked away from the rest of humanity.

He was protecting the world...from him; from what he had become.

Knowing he had no choice, Thomas slowly accepted his new fate, and once he did, he went back inside the cabin to clean it up.

He wasn't like the other man; he wouldn't live like a slob. If he was going to live here in this cabin...alone, he would need to tidy up a bit.

It was as he stepped into the cabin to see what clothes he could find to put on and get to work that he paused and gazed off into the glade where he could see the marker for his wife's grave.

At least he would still have Sharon with him. At least he would still be close to her.

And though many would find their new fate an utter prison, Thomas nodded and smiled, then he entered the cabin to get to work, the door slowly closing behind him.

ANTHONY GIANGREGORIO

HIGHWAY OF THE DEAD

The 405 was clogged with cars, bumper to bumper for the next five miles.

Inside the car, Brad M. Quincy shifted impatiently in his seat, his knuckles white around the steering wheel.

"Damn it, come on," he said for the hundredth time as the lane to his right began moving. All he could do was watch the cars moving by him as he sat idling behind a minivan. Inside the van, a six year old boy stared at him from the rear window. Every time Brad looked forward, the kid would stick out his tongue and make funny faces at him.

At first it was amusing, but now it was just damn annoying.

"Damn kid," he muttered. "Should be in a car seat not jumping around like an idiot."

Checking his watch yet again, he muttered a few choice imprecations. He was going to be late for dinner. And this wasn't just any dinner. It was with his in-laws. Now, normally that wouldn't be so bad, but his in-laws didn't like him very much.

They had a good reason, too. He and his wife had been having marital trouble, the reason obvious to him, but to no one else.

In a nutshell, his wife was a bitch. Yes, that's what he was thinking. His wife was a Grade-A bitch.

You see, whatever he did wasn't good enough for her. Sure, things had been fine when they had first met, but a year later, after the honeymoon was over, she began changing. Everything he did was wrong. He could never please her. And to top it off, she would constantly shit on his dreams of being a writer.

Brad had written three books, but so far they had never left his office at home. She had read them for him, as a good wife should, but to her they were never good enough to put out there in the real world.

Now Brad didn't agree with her. He knew many writers who had put out their own books, all by themselves. It was a new world with new opportunities. Sure, he would be taking a chance his work was good enough, but ask anyone who is a success and they will tell you the same thing. They had to go for it and take that chance. If you don't, then nothing good will ever happen.

Of course, she didn't agree with him and shot him down at every chance she got.

His wife, an English teacher at the local college, was always quick to criticize. Because in her opinion, his books were never good enough, she would constantly belittle him again and again about it.

His plot wasn't well thought or his prose weren't real enough. No matter what he did and what he wrote, she would always knock him back down.

To say she was a negative influence on him was an understatement.

So now, four years after they had tied the knot in a beautiful wedding at the neighborhood church, they were in talks of divorce.

Which was what the dinner was about. Susan's parents were hoping to get it all worked out. They had never liked him anyway and this was their chance to finally get rid of him.

See, his father-in-law was a lawyer and the second he found out about the troubled marriage he'd stuck his nose in their business.

Like father like daughter, huh?

So now he was stuck in traffic and would be late for the dinner. When he got home he knew he was going to hear about it. How he didn't care enough and was selfish, which was why he hadn't come home for dinner on time.

Checking his cell phone for the thousandth time, he saw he was still in a dead zone.

Though cell towers were everywhere, there were still parts of California that didn't have them yet. Especially closer to the outlying mountains which was where he was now.

He shifted lanes, cutting off a grandmother in a blue Toyota, hoping the lane that was moving would now help him.

Glancing in his rearview mirror, he saw the grandmother flipping him off. Her dentures gleamed in the fading sun as her finger saluted him, announcing he was *number 1*.

He shrugged and waved, apologizing, but she just shook her head, annoyed.

No sooner did he straighten out in his new lane, his car now moving past the minivan so he was now side by side with them, then the kid in the van shifted windows, now dragging his mouth over the glass like a blowfish.

Brad ignored this, pretending he was focusing on the car in front of him, and as he silently urged the car in front to move, it then stopped and he watched the minivan begin to crawl forward, soon three cars up and still moving as he sat idle.

"Oh, come on, that ain't right," he snapped as he wiped his brow.

It was warm out, despite the fading sun, and his air conditioning had cut out a week ago and he hadn't wanted to let go of the car to get it fixed. Now he was paying for it as he sat in the warm car roasting like a turkey in an oven set at 475.

Deciding he needed a distraction, he turned on the radio, the station set to the news.

"...and at this time the reports are inconclusive. To reiterate, scenes of mass hysteria are coming in from across the country. No one seems to understand what is happening and reports have been fuzzy as authorities try to make sense of what's happening, but it appears the d..."

"Forget this crap," Brad growled under his breath. It was just more ways the mass media would try to make everyone scared over nothing. He bet it was a few political radicals bitching about the Iraq war again. All the tree huggers wanted it to be over. But, hey, they didn't mind having oil heat their homes did they? They needed gas for their VW vans and Volvos. It's easy to take the high horse when it's not your ass about to get shot off in some Godfor-saken desert country.

Idiots, all of them. They all needed to get a life.

He sat in traffic for another two hours, his body probably sweating out at least a quart of water, but finally he reached the end of the clog and the road opened up once more.

As he passed the reason for the hold up, he wanted to scream with rage and annoyance. Two cars were on the side of the shoulder of the highway and it looked like one had tapped the other by accident. There was no damage to either car, perhaps a scratched bumper if anything, but they had to pull over and change papers for insurance. And the best part was the first car hadn't pulled over enough, so now traffic in that lane had to merge into the middle one. All this shit, all this time wasted, simply because one asshole was too selfish to park correctly in the break down lane.

He honked at them as he passed by, flipping them off. The guy in the second car yelled at Brad and waved his fist but then Brad was gone, shooting down the road and gaining speed with each passing second.

Brad had to wonder what they were waiting for. Were they really waiting for hours for a police car to arrive? Well, that would take a while as the cop was probably stuck in traffic, too. He had seen more than one car on the shoulder in the break down lane, which would mean the squad car wouldn't be able to get by.

It was as he glanced in his mirror at the receding accident that he saw a police car finally arrive. Too late to speed him up, of course, he thought. Figures.

His foot was heavy on the gas as he tried to make up the time he'd lost.

He wasn't the only one. All the cars around him had floored their gas pedals, finally free of the traffic jam. It was like a race track at the start of the race as each car shot forward like a rocket, every single vehicle late for something, no doubt.

Finally, he was making good time as he and the other commuters shot down the highway like rats deserting a sinking ship.

But no sooner did he get a few minutes of freedom, then suddenly every car and truck in front of him seemed to hit the brakes, more than one swerving to the left and right as others began rear ending one another.

Like the classic domino effect, each vehicle crashed into the one in front of it. And when something larger, like a tow truck, or one of those massive SUV's that could be used as tanks in Third World countries, crashed into smaller cars, they crushed them instantly into twisted metal; it was beyond horrible.

Inside those twisted metal vehicles were people, but now they quickly became exploding bags of meat as the bodies were pummeled and battered by the force of the accidents.

One car, a Honda Civic, was struck from behind by a Lincoln Navigator. But the Navigator didn't just rear end the Honda. Instead, with its higher wheel base, it simply ran over the Honda, flattening the roof of the small car and pulverizing the three people inside it. As the Navigator bounced over the car and then rolled onto its side amid a shattering of glass and groaning metal, the Honda began to leak something dark and red out of the bottom of doors, and it most definitely wasn't oil.

Even if the passengers had worn seat beats it wouldn't have mattered, for when a giant hand seems to come out of the sky and swat your car flat like a bug, there's no chance for survival.

Another car rear ended the one in front of it and the impact was so abrupt the driver was catapulted through his windshield, the bloody body flying ten feet into the air before landing heavily on the road. But no sooner did the body land and come to a stop, then another car drove directly over the body, the left tires driving straight through the still form and bifurcating it as easily as if the tires had been blades. The man, now in two parts, was somehow still conscious and he screamed in agony as his intestines slid out of his severed half as he tried to use his one working arm to scoop them back in. His other arm was useless, the ulna bone poking out at an odd angle.

Similar acts of carnage were happening all across the highway as car after car, truck after truck, crashed into one another in what would later be called the largest multiple vehicle pile-up in the past ten years.

Brad felt his car slide as he applied the brakes, and before he knew what was happening, he was upside down and sliding across the pavement, the roof of his car flashing sparks in all directions. As his car spun like a top, he gripped the steering wheel, trying to get the car to do something he wanted it to. Of course being upside down, there was nothing he could do, and if someone had watched him, it would have been amusing to see a car sliding upside down along the highway while the driver tried to steer it, the front tires turning back and forth like a radio controlled car that had been flipped over.

He screamed as the sound of grinding metal filled his ears and then the car spun forward and he saw he was heading right for the pile-up. He only had time for one brief gasp and then his car joined the rest, the airbag deploying and slamming him in the face.

The impact was like a giant had punched him, and before he knew what was happening, he lost consciousness as behind him, more cars and trucks crashed into him, crushing his car into a junkyard mess of steel and fiberglass.

*   *   *

Brad was dreaming.

In his dream, he was at a book signing for his first release, a best seller too. In his dream he had taken a chance and had put out his book by himself, ignoring his wife's complaining, and had been discovered in less than a month.

People loved his book, many wanting to own multiple copies. The book's plot was so original, so ambitious, that all ages, male and female alike, could relate to it.

In less than a month after publishing his book, he was a household name. Fans screamed to see him, wanting his autograph, and of course his book was soon to be made into a major motion picture.

As he sat behind the table signing autographs, the fans lined up out the door and around the block, all wanting to get a glimpse of him, or maybe better, to actually get to talk to him.

Oh, yes, all was right with the world as fans screamed for him, some fighting with others to be next in line. But then the fans grew ugly, battling one another to be next. Soon there was utter chaos and a riot broke out, and before Brad knew it, he was being swallowed by a score of hands and feet as they tried to grab him, wanting a piece of his clothing or a clipping of his hair. But it didn't stop there. Soon they were pulling at his actual body, more than one fan wanting to take the ultimate prize. As he yelled in pain, his arms and legs, his eyelids, ears and nose were ripped away from him as glorious crimson and scarlet fluid sprayed into the fan's faces. But instead of being horrified, they lapped up the blood, wanting to taste his essence, and a few became so aroused they then set in with teeth and fingernails, digging into his chest as more ripped at his throat.

As he gurgled his last shriek of pain, the fans, the ones who were supposed to love him, began to eat him, slowly devouring him alive. It was then that he realized there was a two-edged sword to being discovered, and perhaps it wasn't so bad not publishing his books and remaining anonymous. It might have been better to remain unknown by the public and the opinionated, off balance fans that waited to step on his work and crush his dreams before they could begin.

*   *   *

Brad slowly opened his eyes, not understanding where he was, and for one brief moment he thought he was back in his dream. It sure seemed that way, after all, he could hear people screaming and yelling, sounds of people in agony. In the air was the scent of spilled blood, coppery and sweet, and mixed with it he could detect the scent of gasoline and engine oil, burnt or burning by the smell of it.

Mentally, he did a quick inspection of himself, and as he wiggled his toes and fingers and tried to move his legs, he didn't feel anything was damaged and he didn't cry out in pain. His seatbelt and airbag had saved his life.

Reaching up, as he was upside down, he undid the seatbelt and dropped to the roof of his car, which was now the floor.

Being careful not to cut himself on the safety glass littering the headliner, he began to climb out of the car, wiggling like a worm leaving an apple. When he was halfway out, he wrapped his hand around the window frame and pulled himself the rest of the way.

With his legs still inside the car, he rested for a second. Though muffled, he could hear the cries of people calling for help, but he ignored them. He needed to worry about himself right now.

With his upper body protruding out of the car, he began to feel rain on his neck. But then he realized rain wasn't usually this warm.

Reaching down, he touched the dark liquid on his skin, and when he pulled his hand back to see it, there was blood on his fingers.

Thinking it was his and beginning to panic more than he already was, he glanced above him to see a headless torso draped over the undercarriage of his car, the drip, drip, drip, of the blood coming from the jagged open neck wound where the head should have been.

Crying out in revulsion at the sight of a headless corpse, he scurried the rest of the way out of the window frame and rolled to the side, wanting to distance himself from the sight of the corpse. Then he rested his head and closed his eyes as he thanked God he was still alive. But he didn't stay there for long, the smell of burning vehicles coming to his nose as the sky filled with smoke.

Taking it slow, he went to his knees, a wave of dizziness suffusing him, but then it dissipated, leaving as fast as it had arrived now that blood was pumping throughout his body. Looking around, he still couldn't see anything. The other vehicles around him blocked his view of the rest of the highway and pile-up. But then he spotted one familiar vehicle.

There was a minivan to his left, and as he looked into the shattered rear window, he saw the same child who had been teasing him only minutes before. The boy was now upside down, his arms and legs limp, his eyes staring at nothing. There was a piece of metal in the boy's head, looking like a shark fin. It was embedded in his forehead and Brad had to look away, feeling guilty about what he'd thought about the boy when they had been stuck in traffic.

Stumbling to his feet, he gasped at the overwhelming sight that greeted him.

For hundreds of yards in both directions there was nothing but a sea of twisted metal and steel. Bodies were everywhere, draped over hoods and bumpers and lying on trunks of cars and trucks like they were sunning themselves at the park. An eighteen wheeler was near the back of the pile-up and it had rolled, flattening ten vehicles before it came to a stop. Blood seeped out of the crushed frames, the people inside not just dead but entirely destroyed.

Brad took a few faltering steps, not knowing where to go, and he came upon a station wagon. A family of five was inside, but they were all dead now. The driver, the father, had a four inch round electrical pipe through the middle of his face. The reason for this was the pickup truck he'd rear-ended was carrying the other pipes and electrical supplies now spread out across the pavement.

The children all had broken necks and the wife was hanging out of the fractured windshield, her head almost completely turned around. Her wedding ring flashed in the setting sun and her eyes seeped blood, as if in her last moments on Earth she wept for her lost family.

A man came towards Brad, shambling slowly; hands out in front of him like one of those Frankenstein movies. The eyes were glassy and there was a large wound on his scalp. Slowly, the man shuffled towards Brad, who still hadn't noticed him, too caught up in the visceral carnage of death before him.

Horns blared, small fires popped and crackled, and in the back of the pile-up a vehicle exploded, spraying fire and burning fuel in all directions. If this wasn't Hell on Earth it was a damn good facsimile.

Brad turned when he noticed the shadow of the figure coming up behind him and he spun at the last second to stare into the glossy eyes of the bloody man.

"Please help me, my family, they're trapped in my car back there, please," the bloody man gasped as he reached out for Brad, wrapping his fingers in Brad's shirt.

"Fuck off, buddy, I've got my own problems," Brad said and tore the man's hands away from him, then shoved him away.

The man barely acknowledged the snub, too dazed from the accident to fully understand what was happening. He stumbled away to seek help elsewhere.

Brad stumbled along himself, staring at scenes of death in every direction.

To his left was a jeep and under the front left tire was a baby. The infant couldn't have been more than a month old tops, but now the little one would never see another sunset. The head was nothing but a deflated balloon, the tire having pulverized the small body. One hand was sticking out of the mass of meat, the tiny fingers still holding a rattle with splotches of blood on it.

This was too much for Brad and he leaned over and let his stomach empty its contents across the highway, the hotdog and salad he'd eaten for lunch splashing and then rolling with the slant of the road.

When he could function again, he averted his eyes to prevent another bout and moved on, searching for help, he supposed.

Everywhere he looked there was nothing but suffering. Human arms and legs were strewn about, more than one lone, decapitated head lying on the pavement like a lost soccer ball. The eyes in the heads were always open, the mouths hanging slack in shock or surprise. He couldn't help but wonder what was the last thing they saw before their heads were separated from their shoulders.

He heard another child crying and turned to see a small girl, maybe five. She was covered in blood from head to toe and was calling out for her mommy. Then she turned and wandered in the opposite direction to be lost from sight behind the wreck of a Saab.

"You, there! Hey, you!" a voice called out to his right and Brad at first didn't turn to it. He was so lost in his own world of misery and despair he thought he had stumbled into one of his own worst nightmares. But then the voice called out again, the strong authoritive tone snapping him out of his fugue state.

"I said you, hey, wake the hell up, man! I need some help over here!"

Brad followed the sound of the voice to see a man in between two cars with locked bumpers. The man was hovering over a woman who was sprawled on the road like she'd decided to take a nap.

The man looked up when Brad reached him and he pointed a blood-covered finger at Brad.

"Yes, you! Get your ass over here. I need help if I'm going to be able to save this woman."

Brad did as he was told, moving more on autopilot than an actual want of helping. It was just a thing he did when he didn't know what to do in a situation. If someone else acted like they knew what they were doing, Brad would follow them without question.

Brad was what you would call a *follower*.

When Brad had shuffled a few feet closer to the man, the blood-covered finger pointed down at the woman.

"Come on, get over here! Hurry up, damn you!" he snapped and Brad did as he was told.

"Uh, what do you want?" Brad mumbled.

"Lean down here, I need your hand," the man said. "I'm a doctor and I need to work fast or this woman will die."

Brad knelt down, and when he moved to the side of the doctor, he could now see the woman's upper body.

"She looks pretty dead now. What's the point?"

"Just do as I say, and don't argue with me," the doctor snapped.

Brad did as he was told, though he felt it was a waste of time. To say the woman was a mess would be an understatement. A seven inch long and three inch diameter pipe was sticking out of her chest; right between what Brad would have normally called a great rack. He knew this because her shirt was draped to the side so her entire upper body was exposed. But any sexual excitement was lost when he stared at the pipe jutting out of her chest like a flagpole in a front yard.

Blood seeped from the wound as the doctor tried to save the woman's life.

"The pipe is cutting off her airway. She's got a punctured lung and at least two ribs are completely shattered. I need to remove the pipe so I can reinflate the lung. And I need your help."

"My help? What the hell can I do? I'm not a doctor or a nurse. I'm an accountant for Christ's sake!" Brad snapped back, a little more of himself returning. All around them people were yelling, screaming, wailing, running around, some calling out for loved ones, begging and pleading for someone to help them. A few sirens could be heard as fire and emergency services tried to get to people who could use them, but there were so many it would be hours, maybe days before everyone was helped and found under all the wreckage.

"It doesn't matter what you are, I just need your hands," the doctor said gruffly.

"Fine, what do you want me to do?" Brad asked.

The doctor reached down and grasped the pipe with both hands.

"I'm going to pull this out. When I do I need you to place your hands over the wound or she'll bleed out. I'd let you take the pipe out but it has to be done a certain way, not just yanked out. We clear?" He looked at Brad who was staring down at the woman.

"I said, are we clear?"

"Yes, we're clear, I heard you, shit, I'm not deaf," Brad snapped back.

The doctor nodded and without waiting a second longer, he pulled on the pipe at an angle, sliding it out of the woman's torso.

The woman, who had been unconscious, suddenly woke up from the pain, her mouth opening wide in a guttural cry. Blood shot from her mouth to spray Brad's face and he sputtered as he wiped it away.

"Your hand, get your hand on her wound, dammit!" the doctor screamed as he set the pipe down.

But Brad hesitated, too overcome with shock as the woman stared at him with terror-filled eyes, her pupils as large as quarters. As for where the pipe had been, a geyser of blood shot out of the ghastly opening, a small Old Faithful shooting the plasma straight up. The doctor, disgusted at Brad, dove in and placed a hand over her wound, but no sooner did he do this than the woman began to choke, convulsing as she died, her eyes rolling back into her head and then her lids closing forever.

It wasn't drawn out. One second she was alive, then she was dead, the blood slowing as her heart stopped pumping.

The doctor worked on her frantically, but after a two full minutes he leaned back and sighed, his hands so covered in congealing blood it looked like he was wearing crimson gloves

"Dammit, she's dead." He turned to glare at Brad. "What the fuck is wrong with you, man? I told you to do a simple thing. She bled out in seconds. She'd already lost a lot of blood. She couldn't afford to lose a tablespoon more." He frowned heavily. "Thanks to you she's dead."

Brad's eyes went wide at the man's words. "Whoa, now just back the fucking truck up there, Doctor! Don't try to blame this shit on me. I didn't cause this fucking pile-up. I didn't kill her! Hell, I didn't even want to help in the first place. So you can take your accusing tone and shove it right up your ass!"

"Well, I've never..." the doctor gasped.

"I couldn't give a goddamn what you did or didn't do. Don't make me your scapegoat. The bitch was dead the second that pipe went into her. Anyone with half a brain could see that!"

"My Lord, man, how can you be so heartless? She was a human being for God's sake!"

"Yeah, well, she's nothing but dead meat now, so fuck off and leave me alone!"

Brad got up and turned to walk away and the doctor, still leaning next to the dead woman, looked up to stare at Brad's back.

"It's people like you that make the world what it is!" he called after Brad who ignored him.

It was as the doctor looked back down at the woman, wanting to cover her chest again and give her some dignity in death that the woman's eyes suddenly opened.

The doctor didn't see this, concentrating on buttoning her blood-soaked shirt, but when her head tilted to the side and her mouth opened and closed slightly, he gasped in amazement.

"Good God, she's still alive!" he cried and reached down to check her pulse to see how strong it was. It was as he reached his hand to her throat that she suddenly turned her head and raised it, her left arm coming up, her hand grasping the doctor's wrist.

"What are you...?" was all the doctor got out before the previously dead woman sank her teeth into his wrist, tearing out a two inch chunk of his flesh.

The doctor screamed and pushed her away, punching her in the head with his free hand. It was instinct, something he would have never do on normal circumstances, but as her teeth came away with a chunk of his arm and his blood shot out to bathe her face like syrup, he found himself not worrying about etiquette and only worrying about himself.

Brad had walked a ways a bit and he now turned around to glance over his shoulder to see what the doctor was yelling about.

Brad was about to tell the guy to fuck off once and for all, but when his eyes locked onto the man and the prone woman, things didn't look the same as when he'd left them a few moments ago.

It looked like the woman was moving, as impossible as that seemed, and the doctor seemed to be bent over her.

Mildly curious as to what was going on, he spun about and jogged back to them, and when he reached the doctor and peered over his shoulder, his mouth fell open at the sight before him.

The dead woman had managed to get her teeth into the doctor's throat and now was chewing like a dog on a meat bone. The doctor was helpless, locked in her grip, as both of the woman's hands held his head firmly between them.

"Jesus Christ! What the fuck is going on here!" Brad yelled, astonished at this graphic scene that made absolutely no sense. It was amazing that the woman was alive, but more than a little odd that the first thing she would want to do is eat the man who had saved her.

The doctor's throat was shooting blood and he managed to pull his head free of her grasp and stand up. As he did this, blood geysered out of his torn jugular to splash Brad with warm gore.

"What the hell? Holy shit!" Brad screamed, having no idea what to do. His legs were frozen as he watched the doctor stumble away to then fall onto the road, his arms and legs twitching as blood spilled out onto the pavement.

Brad's mouth was hanging open and he could taste the doctor's blood on his tongue. He didn't know what to do. In the back of his mind he began hearing more screams and yells, but they sounded different now, more terror added to the tones.

And then his eyes went back to the prone woman who was even now sitting up, her face and upper chest covered in the doctor's warm blood, the plasma mixing with her own congealed blood covering her breasts. Her mounds of glory swayed back and forth and Brad found his eyes going to them, but then his eyes went higher and he saw her chewing on the doctor's skin. She swallowed the flesh and then hissed at him, Brad taking a step back, not understanding what he should do.

Should he run? Should he try to help her? He'd seen what the doctor did when he tried to help her and he didn't want to end up like that.

The woman crawled on her knees and then stood up, using a nearby car for support. When she was standing, there was that circular hole in her chest which allowed light to seep through like a peep hole. She began stepping toward Brad.

Brad's mouth dropped so low it seemed to scrape the road as he stared at this woman who should definitely be dead. The hole in her torso was perfectly round and as he watched, he saw people running around behind her. He was using the hole like a telescope!

And then she lunged at him, her hands grabbing his arms as her teeth clacked an inch from his face.

"Get away from me, you crazy bitch!" Brad snapped as he shoved her away. She was smaller than him and she was pushed back, but then she was at it again.

Brad, out of patience, realizing whatever was happening was so off the charts of reality it couldn't be rational, waited for her to come at him again, and this time he punched her squarely in the chin. The woman's head rocked back and her jaw dislocated, the lower half hanging like an old swing, but still she came for him again.

"I'm warning you, lady, try it again and I will clean your clock." He looked around to see if anyone was around who could help him but there was no one. Everyone else was dealing with their own worlds of misery and death.

The dead woman didn't listen and came for him again and this time Brad decided that was it.

As she charged him, albeit slowly, he dodged away from her and scooped up the pipe lying on the ground. The same one she had been impaled with.

Spinning, she hissed again, her lower jaw now resembling an old necktie, her tongue mimicking the jaw. Brad waited for her to come forward again.

"Okay, I warned you," he said firmly, and when she stumbled forward at him, he raised the pipe and whacked her on the side of the head.

Once more her head rocked to the side, and this time when she turned it back to Brad, he saw a large gash on her cheek. Bone could be seen peeking through and the sides of her molars were now visible, but if the woman cared she didn't show it.

"Son of a bitch," Brad gasped as he stepped away from her.

Gargling her ire, the woman came for him again, but Brad had had enough and he decided there were two choices. Run or kill her.

Running was easier and wouldn't land him in jail for killing her, so he turned and was about to run when he found himself face to face with the doctor. The same doctor who had died moments ago from blood loss.

But the doctor's eyes weren't as clear as before, now they were vacant, dead of emotion and personality.

As Brad stopped cold, the doctor wrapped his arms around him in a bear hug and tried to sink his teeth into his throat.

Screaming, Brad tried to break free and then felt the woman come up against him from behind. Her breasts pushed against his back and even in his terror he felt their softness. But when her face went to his and she tried to bite his ear off, he screamed yet again.

She couldn't do it; however, her lower jaw useless and she seemed to kind of rub her tongue and upper teeth on his face. Blood and saliva was left behind and Brad felt his stomach heaving as he fought for his life.

The doctor turned to bite him again, teeth coming so close they might have taken a chuck out of him, and Brad managed to elude his advance. Then he got his right arm free, the one still holding the pipe.

When the doctor tried again to taste his flesh, Brad brought up the pipe and jammed it into the doctor's left eye. He would never have done this normally, but in his panic he just acted, and as the pipe slid into the socket, scraping bone, he could already feel the revulsion for what he'd done.

The pipe slid almost five inches deep before hanging up on the socket, the doctor falling away from him, releasing Brad. The body hit the pavement hard and the doctor's head whacked with suck force it cracked. As brains seeped out of the fracture and also out of the tip of the pipe like ground hamburger, Brad threw up, coating his shoes with bile and whatever remained in his stomach from his last bout of sickness.

He shoved the dead woman away as he was vomiting and fell backwards to trip over her legs, falling to the road like a drunk. Brad, not wanting to deal with anymore of this shit, picked himself up and stumbled away, wiping his mouth as he went.

If things had been bad at the pileup before, then they were downright hellish now. Everywhere he looked the people he'd seen that had been dead, the kid in the minivan, the family in the station wagon, the man with the pipe in him, all of them were now moving about.

As impossible as it seemed, these people, who had most defiantly been dead, were now up and about and seemed to be searching for the survivors.

Wherever Brad looked, the people who had managed to live through the crash and had been helping others, were now set upon by the victims who had been dead only moments ago.

Brad saw a man pulled down by three children covered with what were obviously mortal wounds, one child having half its chest torn out when it had gone through the windshield of a car. Intestines hung like garland from the boy's abdomen to slap the ground as he moved. Screams filled the air, a symphony of death no man should ever want to hear and Brad stood in the middle of it, watching with dumbstruck eyes.

His throat stung a little, and when he reached up to touch it he felt warm blood. But it wasn't old blood, this was fresh. Feeling with his fingers, he found a wound there, a small bite. But it wasn't life threatening so he ignored it.

Three more dead people popped up behind a squished Volvo and Brad backed away as the undead crawled over the hood of the car.

He knew whatever was happening was so very wrong and he also knew he needed to go...now!

Turning, he ran to the shoulder of the road and began running down the highway, sometimes having to climb over cars that blocked his way. To his right was the guardrail and to his left was the massive pile-up of twisted wreckage and human bodies.

As he ran, he glanced to his left to see people now attacking people. One living dead guy with an arm missing, the other hanging by a few tendons and flesh, was snapping at an old woman like his head was a chicken's. But instead of coming back with bird seed in his beak, his mouth would pop up with a piece of the old woman's face.

Carnage was everywhere and as Brad ran, the sun began to disappear on the horizon, casting the entire scene in a pallid, otherworldly gloom that just made it seem all the more preposterous.

He felt himself growing tired and when he raised his hand to his throat to inspect his wound again, he felt the blood still flowing.

It looked like the doctor had gotten a piece of him after all.

Eventually he made it to the top of the wreck, where the first car had sideswiped another vehicle, causing the cascade of death and destruction, and as he slowed, he saw there were a few cars at the point that weren't in the wreck. These cars were from people who had seen what was happening in their rearview mirrors and had stopped to then drive back to assist in saving lives.

That was fine with Brad, for now one of these cars was going to save his life.

He found an old, beat up Chevy, the engine still running, and he hopped in. He didn't know where the owner was and didn't care, all he knew was he wanted away from this place.

Slamming the transmission into drive, he took off like a rocket, his eyes going to the rearview mirror.

Behind him, what was visible was the walking dead chomping on the living, a feast of meat and internal organs that would rival any horror movie. He heard the sounds of rotors beating the night sky and glanced up into the night sky to see three helicopters approaching the massive accident, the spotlights already lighting up the night.

He didn't care about them, about any of it. None of it was his problem anymore.

Stepping on the gas pedal harder, he drove off into the night. Though he felt woozy, not understanding that he was losing blood at an alarming rate and would die of blood loss if he didn't get medial assistance fast, he headed home for the dinner date with his wife and in-laws,

* * *

By the time Brad reached the street his house was on, he was as white as a ghost and could barely see the road in front of him. Thinking it was foggy, he put the high beams on, but it did little to help his situation.

His mind was fuzzy, his reactions were slow, and he sideswiped more than one parked car on his way home. But there were no police out this night, as every available officer was back at the massive pile-up on the highway.

It was as he approached his home, only a few doors down, that his vision finally began to fade.

His will was so strong that he forced himself awake and managed to swing the Chevy into his driveway, but no sooner did the front tires touch the asphalt, then his head slumped forward, he closed his eyes, and passed out, seconds later descending into death.

The front bumper of the Chevy ended up hitting the garage door, but with Brad's foot now releasing the gas pedal, the car only tapped it, barely scratching the paint on the roll up door and pushing the door in les than an inch.

The Chevy sat idling, the garage door preventing it from wanting to move, and Brad's still body remained that way for another ten minutes.

The man was clinically dead, his clothing saturated with blood, a few points adding to the grime of the filthy seat of the Chevy.

Nothing stirred in the neighborhood except for a few barking dogs in nearby yards who wanted to be let inside, but then, inside the Chevy, one of Brad's fingers began to twitch.

Soon, the rest of the fingers were moving, and then Brad opened his eyes and sat up, his head coming up solely, like he was underwater.

His hands reached out, flailing, and his thumb hit the ON button for the radio, turning it on. An announcer was droning on about the massive pile-up out on the 405 and how the scene of a tragic and terrible series of accidents had transformed the crash site into a riot, with the people who had suffered injuries now attacking the rescue workers and anyone close to them. The state police had been called to the scene in force and were even now rounding up the attackers. It was also added that the National Guard had been called in to make sure things didn't get out of control.

Reports were still sketchy, but the news station had been hearing reports of people being shot and killed who wouldn't stand down. More information would be told when it came in.

Brad never heard any of it, his ears now feeling like they were stuffed with cotton.

His dead mind remembered one thing, however.

He had a date, a dinner date to attend.

A hand that felt like mush managed to open the driver's door after a few trial and errors and Brad stepped out into the driveway, swaying back and forth like he was drunk. In the darkness of the street, his clothing didn't look so bad, the crimson stains blending in with the original color of his shirt.

His eyes shifted in his head and then rested on his front door a few feet away.

Stumbling like a drunkard, he made his way to the front stoop and reached out for the door handle.

There was no elation, no pleasing thoughts as he squeezed the handle and opened the door. It had been unlocked hours ago by his wife in anticipation of him returning home.

As he stepped into the foyer, the lights were off, but the living and dining room lights were on high, thus casting the foyer into even darker shadows than by those standing in the brighter part of the house.

As the door closed behind Brad, voices could be heard, dishes and silverware clinking and clanking as everyone seated at the table got up at once and moved into the foyer.

Brad stood by the door, the shadows of the foyer hiding his pale complexion and blood-stained clothes.

As one, his wife and her parents appeared at the opposite end of the house and stared at him standing there quietly.

"Well, Brad, aren't you going to come in and say hello to my folks?" his wife asked arrogantly.

She had always been the power in the relationship and he had always kowtowed to her, never being a man and standing up for himself.

His father-in-law took a few a steps forward into the foyer. He didn't have his glasses on so Brad appeared to be nothing but a blur.

"Well, son, aren't you going to say hello? You know what? Forget it; let's not waste time with pleasantries. You know why I'm here so there's no reason to dance around it. Because you didn't bother to show me any respect by being on time for dinner I'll just lay it out for you. I want an answer to the question you've already been asked. Which is, are you going to give my daughter a divorce?"

"Uhm, Daddy, I don't think Brad's all right. I think there's something wrong with him," she said as she tried to see into the dark foyer.

"Nonsense, he's perfectly fine. He's just stalling," her father said and then turned back to Brad. "So, son, what's your answer? Are you going to give her what she wants or what?

That's when Brad lunged forward, sinking his teeth into his father-in-law's throat, tearing out the man's carotid artery as he sucked in the warm plasma. It felt fantastic and it filled him with strength as the warm fluid slid down his throat.

As he chewed merrily, he gazed over the man's twitching shoulder to see his wife and mother-in-law standing there in utter shock. Brad let go of his father-in-law, the man slumping to the floor dead. But that was all right, he would be up soon enough.

As he took one faltering step towards his wife, he actually managed a slight grin, his dull brain thinking about what his father-in-law had just said about giving it to his wife.

Oh, yes, he was going to give it to her, but not a divorce. Instead he was going to give her everlasting life...as one of the undead.

Lunging forward, he grabbed her by the hair and sank his teeth into her cheek, tearing her skin from her face like it was the skin of a roasted chicken. No sooner did he do this then he went for her throat, the thin, swan like neck that had so aroused him when they had been dating now torn to shreds.

And as his teeth sank into her ivory flesh, she screamed, and he relished it. For once he was in charge and would stay that way for all eternity.

When he was through with her he would then take care of his mother-in-law, but for now he was savoring his victory over his shrew of a wife.

Their screams filled the house and floated into the street, but no one heard them as the other homes on the street had their own screams as the walking dead slowly swarmed into the neighborhood to attack the living.

As he fed on his wife's spasming body and she succumbed to death, she let out one ear-piercing scream before the same screams were swallowed by gargling noises as she drowned in blood.

To Brad, it was music to his undead ears.

ABOUT THE WRITERS

Anthony Giangregorio is the author of more than 20 novels, almost all of them about zombies. His work has appeared in *Dead Science* by Coscomentertainment, *Dead Worlds: Undead Stories Volumes 1, 2 &, 3, Book of the Dead*, and an upcoming anthology (Zombology) by Library of the Living Dead Press and their werewolf anthology titled *War Wolves*.

Check out his website at www.undeadpress.com

Joseph Giangregorio is nineteen years old. He co-wrote the zombie book *Visions of the Dead* with his father and has a story in the zombie anthology *Dead Worlds: Undead Stories, Volume 2.*

He is presently attending college for his associates degree and from there will be moving on to his bachelors. He's also a promising welder who is in the process of becoming certified.

Domenic Giangregorio is twelve years old, and when he's not writing stories with his father, he's playing video games and just having fun being a kid.

REVOLUTION OF THE DEAD
By Anthony Giangregorio
THE DEAD SHALL RISE AGAIN!

Five years ago, a deadly plague wiped out 97% of the world's population, America suffering tragically. Bodies were everywhere, far too many to bury or burn. But then, through a miracle of medical science, a way is found to reanimate the dead.

With the manpower of the United States depleted, and the remaining survivors not wanting to give up their internet and fast food restaurants, the undead are conscripted as slave labor.

Now they cut the grass, pick up the trash, and walk the dogs of the surviving humans.

But whether alive or dead, no race wants to be controlled, and sooner or later the dead will fight back, wanting the freedom they enjoyed in life.

The revolution has begun!

And when it's over, the dead will rule the land, and the remaining humans will become the slaves...or worse.

DEAD RECKONING: DAWNING OF THE DEAD
By Anthony Giangregorio
THE DEAD HAVE RISEN!

In the dead city of Pittsburgh, two small enclaves struggle to survive, eking out an existence of hand to mouth.

But instead of working together, both groups battle for the last remaining fuel and supplies of a city filled with the living dead.

Six months after the initial outbreak, a lone helicopter arrives bearing two more survivors and a newborn baby. One enclave welcomes them, while the other schemes to steal their helicopter and escape the decaying city.

With no police, fire, or social services existing, the two will battle for dominance in the steel city of the walking dead. But when the dust settles, the question is: will the remaining humans be the winners, or the losers?

When the dead walk, the line between Heaven and Hell is so twisted and bent there is no line at all.

RISE OF THE DEAD
by Anthony Giangregorio
DEATH IS ONLY THE BEGINNING!

In less than forty-eight hours, more than half the globe was infected.

In another forty-eight, the rest would be enveloped.

The reason?

A science experiment gone horribly wrong which enabled the dead to walk, their flesh rotting on their bones even as they seek human prey.

Jeremy was an ordinary nineteen year old slacker. He partied too much and had done poorly in high school. After a night of drinking and drugs, he awoke to find the world a very different place from the one he'd left the night before.

The dead were walking and feeding on the living, and as Jeremy stepped out into a world gone mad, the dead spotting him alone and unarmed in the middle of the street, he had to wonder if he would live long enough to see his twentieth birthday.

DEADFREEZE
By Anthony Giangregorio

THIS IS WHAT HELL WOULD BE LIKE IF IT FROZE OVER!

When an experimental serum for hypothermia goes horribly wrong, a small research station in the middle of Antarctica becomes overrun with an army of the frozen dead.

Now a small group of survivors must battle the arctic weather and a horde of frozen zombies as they make their way across the frozen plains of Antarctica to a neighboring research station.

What they don't realize is that they are being hunted by an entity whose sole reason for existing is vengeance; and it will find them wherever they run.

DEAD WORLDS: Undead Stories
A Zombie Anthology Volume 1
Edited by Anthony Giangregorio

Welcome to the world of the dead, where the laws of nature have been twisted, reality changed.

The Dead Walk!

Filled with established and promising new authors for the next generation of corpses, this anthology will leave you gasping for air as you go from one terror-filled story to another.

Like the decomposing meat of a freshly rotting carcass, this book will leave you breathless.

Don't say we didn't warn you.

VISIONS OF THE DEAD
A ZOMBIE STORY
By Anthony & Joseph Giangregorio

Jake Roberts felt like he was the luckiest man alive.

He had a great family, a beautiful girlfriend, who was soon to be his wife, and a job, that might not have been the best, but it paid the bills.

At least until the dead began to walk.

Now Jake is fighting to survive in a dead world while searching for his lost love, Melissa, knowing she's out there somewhere.

But the past isn't dead, and as he struggles for an uncertain future, the past threatens to consume him.

With the present a constant battle between the living and the dead, Jake finds himself slipping in and out of the past, the visions of how it all happened haunting him.

But Jake knows Melissa is out there somewhere and he'll find her or die trying. In a world of the living dead, you can never escape your past.

DEAD WORLDS: Undead Stories
A Zombie Anthology Volume 2
Edited by Anthony Giangregorio

Welcome to a world where the dead walk and want nothing more than to feast on the living.

The stories contained in this, the second volume of the Dead Worlds series, are filled with action, gore, and buckets and buckets of blood; plus a heaping side of entrails for those with a little extra hunger.

The stories contained within this volume are scribed by both the desiccated cadavers of seasoned veterans to the genre as well as fresh-faced corpses, each printed here for the first time; and all of them ready to dig in and please the most discerning reader.

So slap on a bib and prepare to get bloody, because you're about to read the best zombie stories this side of Hell!

THE DARK
By Anthony Giangregorio
DARKNESS FALLS

The darkness came without warning.

First New York, then the rest of United States, and then the world became enveloped in a perpetual night without end.

With no sunlight, eventually the planet will wither and die, bringing on a new Ice Age. But that isn't problem for the human race, for humanity will be dead long before that happens.

There is something in the dark, creatures only seen in nightmares, and they are on the prowl. Evolution has changed and man is no longer the dominant species. When we are children, we're told not to fear the dark, that what we believe to exist in the shadows is false.

Unfortunately, that is no longer true.

BOOK OF THE DEAD
A Zombie Anthology

You now hold in your hands the most faithful, truest zombie anthology ever written and we invite you along for the ride.

Every single story in this book is filled with slack-jawed, eyes glazed, slow moving, shambling zombies set in a world where the dead have risen and only want to eat the flesh of the living.

In these pages, the rules are sacrosanct. There is no deviation from what a zombie should be or how they came about.

The Dead Walk.

There is no reason, though rumors and suppositions fill the radio and television stations. But the only thing that is fact is that the walking dead are here and they will not go away.

So prepare yourself for the ultimate homage to the master of zombie legend. And remember... *Aim for the head!*

SEE HOW IT ALL BEGAN IN THE NEW DOUBLE-SIZED EDITION!
DEADWATER: EXPANDED EDITION
By Anthony Giangregorio

Through a series of tragic mishaps, a small town's water supply is contaminated with a deadly bacterium that transforms the town's population into flesh eating ghouls.

Without warning, Henry Watson finds himself thrown into a living hell where the living dead walk and want nothing more than to feed on the living.

Now Henry's trying to escape the undead town before he becomes the next victim.

With the military on one side, shooting civilians on sight, and a horde of bloodthirsty zombies on the other, Henry must try to battle his way to freedom.

With a small group of survivors, including a beautiful secretary and a wise-cracking janitor to aid him, the ragtag group will do their best to stay alive and escape the city codenamed: **Deadwater.**

DEAD END: A ZOMBIE NOVEL
By Anthony Giangregorio
THE DEAD WALK!

Newspapers everywhere proclaim the dead have returned to feast on the living!

A small group of survivors hole up in a cellar, afraid to brave the masses of animated corpses, but when food runs out, they have no choice but to venture out into a world gone mad.

What they will discover, however, is that the fall of civilization has brought out the worst in their fellow man.

Cannibals, psychotic preachers and rapists are just some of the atrocities they must face.

In a world turned upside down, it is life that has hit a Dead End.

DEAD RAGE
By Anthony Giangregorio

An unknown virus spreads across the globe, turning ordinary people into bloodthirsty, ravenous killers.

Only a small percentage of the population is immune and soon become prey to the infected.

Amongst the infected comes a man, stricken by the virus, yet still retaining his grasp on reality. His need to destroy the *normals* becomes an obsession and he raises an army of killers to seek out and kill all who aren't *changed* like himself.

A few survivors gather together on the outskirts of Chicago and find themselves running for their lives as the specter of death looms over all.

The Dead Rage virus will find you, no matter where you hide.

9 781935 458227